# Knowing Self Through Karmayoga

# Knowing Self Through Karmayoga

**Veenaa Ahluwalia**

PRABHAT
PRAKASHAN

*Published by*
**PRABHAT PRAKASHAN PVT. LTD.**
4/19 Asaf Ali Road,
New Delhi-110 002 (INDIA)
e-mail: prabhatbooks@gmail.com

ISBN 978-81-945109-2-5
**KNOWING SELF THROUGH KARMAYOGA**
*by* Smt. Veenaa Ahluwalia

*Edition*
2025

*Price*
₹ 400.00 (Rupees Four Hundred only)



*Printed at*
R-Tech Offset Printers, Delhi

There are reasons for everything and no coincidences exist on the path of destiny. Sometimes it takes a tragedy or a great loss to remind us that life has something else stored for us in the guise of the tragedy.

**Neha**

My Guardian Angel

**(1982-1986)**

I am extremely grateful to my daughter Neha, who came into my life but died very young, opening my mind to the concept of past *karmas*. And to break my *karmic* chain, Neha, you took me to the path of *bhakti*. You are truly my spiritual guide as you helped me to come up in life the spiritual way.

True love is what we carry from life to life. Thank you Mummy and Daddy for being such wonderful parents.

Maa, you were my first *Guru*.

**India**

**My *Janmabhoomi***

I love my country where the *Vedas*, the *Upanishads* and the *Gita* were written; the land where great *rishis and maharishis* were born.

AND

**Dubai**

**My *Karmabhoomi***

(for the last 40 years)

**'A HEAVEN ON EARTH'**

Pujya Swami Chidanand Saraswatiji

Extremely grateful to Swamiji for introducing me to myself.

First copy of this book is dedicated to my grandson,

**VIVHAN**

# Acknowledgements

It is very important to pay serious attention to incidents and events in our lives. There is so much to learn from them. My children, Ashit and Ritu, took me to the path of selfless *karma*.

There is a perfect bond between my husband and me as we both share the same basic principles of life. Thank you, Sunil, for giving me the space to take some important decisions in life. Without your moral support and motivation, this book would not have been possible.

People are wonderful mirrors to help us see our subconscious thought pattern and grow. All my relatives and friends in Dubai for the last 40 years helped me a lot in the transformation of my life. They all gave me many opportunities to observe my inner consciousness. I am grateful to all of them.

A very big 'thank you' to Dr Rajeev Kumar, whose efforts, help and guidance provided in the publication of this book is highly appreciated.

# Introduction

I have written this book to give back a little of what has been given to me. When I thought of penning down my experiences on my journey towards spirituality, I was not sure how I was going to express the depth of my feelings, my inner journey, on the pages of my book. Trust me, it was God Himself, who held my hand and made me write this book. Without divine help, it was not possible for me to express my inner self.

Without the inspiration of God, this book would never have been written. For me God is simple. For me God is love. I do not want to project God as complicated in my book. For me God is TRUST, a complete surrender. Faith in God can produce miracles as had happened in my case.

I remember, in the year 1999, for the first time, an inexplicable event occurred. In the middle of the night, or in the early morning hours, I woke up to find loss of control over myself. I realised that my physical body had lost its heaviness and I felt dead for a few seconds. My body temperature dropped to zero and I felt lifeless for a few seconds. It took mc 10-15 minutes before my blood pressure reached 60-90. I became terribly scared and nervous. I prayed to God for His kindness towards me. Then suddenly, I started seeing flashes of light everywhere in the room—on the wall, on the floor. These lights disturbed me as I didn't know from where these lights were coming! I had no idea! I found myself in a state of fear and semi-psychosis. As was to be expected, I immediately sought medical help. The doctor's report said that I was more than normal. After my first out-of-body experience, I wondered if my life would ever be the same again.

My time to leave this earth had apparently not arrived. My out-of-body experience became a regular feature. Instead of pondering over this mysterious experience, which was beyond words, I started living with it. There was no choice. I had to cope with it as it was an inner experience which had nothing to do with the outer world. At this stage I realised that unknowingly I had becoming meditative and found myself going into a trance very often. I also became very calm and peaceful internally and the flashes of light no longer disturbed me. I started living with it as I was unable to understand why this was happening to me. I never thought of consulting anybody nor approached any *guru*. I completely surrendered myself to God; more prayers, more lights and more out-of-body experiences. I was unable to understand this miracle of God till I met Pujya Swami Chidanand Saraswatiji of Parmarth Niketan Ashram in Rishikesh, by chance, on 30 November, 2011. I had gone there for Ganga *aarti*. Swami Chidanand Saraswatiji asked me and my husband to join him in the *ashram*. In front of many disciples and dignitaries, he explained to me who I was. After my meeting with Pujya Swami Chidanand Saraswatiji, something miraculous happened and I became even more comfortable with the flashes of light and out-of-body experiences, as I started praying more as advised by Saraswatiji.

Once I became comfortable with my experiences, I began to feel as though I had acquired more wisdom and insight and felt gracious at these holy experiences. I was aware that after awakening of the *kundalini,* irrespective of the out-of-body experiences, they often find that their life has been transformed in a positive manner. Physical and emotional healing happens dramatically. The meaning of one's life becomes clearer. I felt my body and mind had become aligned. Healing occurs as the mind gets attuned to the body.

The body starts receiving signals on do's and don'ts. Everything became clear as I felt as if I had attained *gyana*. Through this *gyana,* our *karma* becomes *nishkam karma* and our *bhakti* becomes pure *bhakti*. We become clairvoyant, more aware and more alert. This state can induce a permanent awakening in the true nature of reality. After the awakening of the *kundalini,* some can access information, not normally available through the five senses. There is a sixth sense, which facilitates understanding of the inner world.

Our awareness of God becomes perpetual and does not depend on any particular state of mind. Externally one looks the same, behaves the same, but the inner world gets totally transformed.

In a society, with a misguided concept of God and no tradition of *gurus* or masters, one becomes responsible for setting one's own choices. The choices we make shape our lives. Then we put our hard work, commitment and conviction in these choices. When I lost my daughter Neha, to emerge out of the depression, my mother advised me to adopt the *bhakti marg*. The result was very satisfactory. I can assure you that by leading a perfect *grihastha jeevan*, spirituality can be attained.

A true *karmayogi* engages in worldly activities with care, as he aims to improve the outer world and in the process attains *gyana*— the ability to know self automatically and effortlessly.

Knowing self is not a very easy process; it needs time and strict discipline. It takes years to know self, but God can gift His true devotee a thousand resources to know self. If we are close to God and are spiritually inclined, our physical wealth, that is, health, will automatically come our way.

God is drawn by the magnetic passion in the devotee's range of consciousness, which abounds in intense *bhakti* and *shradha* that pull God with an irresistible force. God bestows the divine experiences of cosmos consciousness when His *Bhakt*, by meditation and *bhakti,* has strengthened his mind to a degree, when the *sakshatkar* does not overwhelm him; only awareness, meditation and *bhakti* can prepare a *bhakt* to absorb the *sakshatkar* of His omnipresence.

During a spiritual *teerthyatra* to Kailash Mansarovar in June 2017, I had no idea that a mesmerising and beautiful experience awaited me. Lord Shiva, in His meditative posture, gave me *darshan* at the Nepalganj airport before we could start our *yatra*. I am an ardent devotee of Lord Shiva.

We were in a group of nearly 50 *teerthyatris*. On reaching Mansarovar Lake, we bathed in the lake and participated in the *Rudrabhishek puja* and *havan*. Everyone was amazed at the arrangement for the *havan.* A real grand *rudra abhishek* and *havan* were performed by all of us, with each of us offering *aahuti.* Then we reached our mud huts and had dinner. Ashwini and Manju (good friends in the group) told my husband Sunil and me to get up early at 3 a.m. to witness the *jyoti*, as it was a full-moon night. At 3 a.m. we went and stood outside our huts facing Mansarovar Lake in a below-zero-degree temperature.

Suddenly, I found myself sinking into a deep meditative state. At this point, I felt I was becoming different; becoming independent. I started staring deep into the sky. I felt the voices of other people and my husband Sunil recede farther and farther away. My body became loose and I surrendered. Suddenly I noticed, on top of my head, that the sky was full of beautiful and bright stars. Stars shone beautifully just above my head. After a while I noted that on my left side, two round lights (size of a saucer plate) began to appear, one after another, moving very, very slowly. The most precious, mesmerising sight was of two round lights in white silvery colour, moving very slowly from the sky and enter into the Mansarovar Lake. Oh God! I was mesmerised, dismayed! I felt as if my soul had made a sudden arrival. I emerged from my meditative state and from the trance. I opened my eyes. I was very calm but moved by my experience. Till date, I have kept my entire experience a very private secret. There is nothing comparable to it in my physical world. My soul knows that this precious light exists and it has existed always. The soul must align with *paramatma,* the Brahman.

The earth is not really our true home. We are here to learn, to grow wise. We are spiritual beings. What we learn here, we take with us when we die; the remaining—materialism, relations, acquaintances remain behind on this earth. Be firm about rejecting the outer world pressure and any criticism over and over again.

I have no doctrine to teach the philosophy of *Bhagvad Gita,* but for me there is only one philosophy and that is *karmayoga,* which is the only solution to all the problems in life. This is the key for self-transformation. Approaching and following *karmayoga,* experientially rather than theoretically, is what Lord Krishna described in the *Gita* and it is a very sophisticated science.

We are here to learn, not to suffer. Why should we suffer? Loss of my child led me to emptiness, sadness, which took me to God (the lasting happiness). When we face any crisis, a personal loss, our attitude towards life changes and we are forced to self-analyse as this helps us and a real change occurs within.

I don't know much about scriptures and techniques; all I know is about myself and my inner journey—from nowhere to knowing God. I was greatly inspired by *Gita's* philosophy of *karmayoga.*

Arjuna harboured certain notions, beliefs and values, because of his attachment to his family, friends and relatives.

He was caught between the duality of attraction and aversion to war and its consequences. Therefore, he experienced anguish and *vishada*.

If we face difficulties in our life, it is possible to come out of our suffering without going to any *guru* or *satsang* because we understand the *Gita*; we live the *Gita*. The *Gita* gives its practitioners the assurance that they can deal with the problems of moral existence with faith and devotion to God and detached from *karma*. There is no need to believe in this blindly. Once we become convinced of what is mentioned in the *Gita* as true, we should incorporate it in our daily life as early as possible. The philosophy of the *Gita* is about the search for serenity, meaningfulness and permanence in a world of rapid changes and how to integrate spiritual values into our ordinary life.

Memorising the *Gita* is not very important; understanding the *Gita* is important. When every action, every gesture of ours indicates the philosophy of the *Gita*, it means that we have understood the *Gita*.

Today, we look for solutions to maintain our well-being, but we have forgotten the true meaning of the philosophy of the *Bhagvad Gita*. The *Gita* is an art that shows how to enjoy life while staying spiritual.

Lord Krishna Himself explained in detail about Himself, the *soul* and *nature* and how they are inter-related.

The *Gita's* main essence and essential message is: how advance and hi-tech we may become, we cannot escape the *karmaphal*. To understand this, we must believe in living the *Gita*, rather than merely reading what is written in it. Living the *Gita* increases our understanding, otherwise what is the point of reading and debating on scriptures? Memorising the *Gita* will not help us; implying, living and practicing *Gita's* philosophy on a daily basis will enlighten us to the fact that one who does good deeds will never come to a bad end—either here, or in the life to come.

To understand this, we don't need to go to the Himalayas.

A *sannyasi* will remain the same even in the Himalayas if he is unable to control his 'senses'. The point lies not in changing the place; the real point lies in changing the inner state of our mind. In today's world, a true *sannyasi* is one who makes life a little more beautiful, more nourished so as to rejoice in life. There is absolutely no need to renounce anything if we know the real meaning of *sannyas*.

True spirituality can make us fully intoxicated without a drop of alcohol. I have never touched liquor in my life, but I know what intoxication is. Once we are spiritually inclined, our brain manufactures happy hormones through meditation and prayers. These happy hormones have an amazing impact on our health and well-being. I believe everything comes at a price. If we waste our time and energy, life does not give us back much in return. My driving ambition is to make each moment count. When the time comes to go, I want to look around with satisfaction.

Man arrives penniless in this world and departs without taking anything from this world. The length of one's life is not important; the number of days and years one lives in one's life is insignificant. It is the quality of these days and years that is important.

We should avoid imposing our ideas on others; instead change our life in such a way that people are forced to NOTICE. An incredibly beautiful soul can be differentiated from the crowd—this is the essence of spirituality, of grace and of sophistication. It is the most amazing experience and anyone can experience it.

This book provides simple but comprehensive ways to deal with all aspects of human behaviour, problems and solutions. This book is neither preachy nor meant to impart serious lectures. I am not trying to advocate something which is difficult and unachievable. You just have to come out of your comfort zone. I hope you find this book inviting, as it helps in awakening consciousness, which is what spirituality is all about. Spirituality is not an object of our search; it is about searching our self. There are still choices and it is not too late to make them.

***—Veenaa Ahluwalia***

# Contents


*Acknowledgements* 7

*Introduction* 9

**1. Beginning** **25**

Our Choice is Our *Karma* 28

Our *Karma* Today Defines Our Future Tomorrow 29

Debts must be Paid 33

*Karma* is to Learn from Our Wrongdoings 33

The *Karmic* Chain 34

Ways to Break the *Karmic* Chain 37

**2. Karmayoga** **41**

*Karmic* Seeds 50

Negative (Dark) Seeds 51

Intention 73

Positive Seeds 76

Conscious Efforts to Avoid Bad *Karmic* Seeds 78

Loving Nature is a Positive *Karma* 86

Be environment-friendly 87

Collective *Karma* 87

*Karma* in Relationship 88

3. **Bhaktiyoga** **95**

Logic In *Bhakti* 104

God is Gracious 106

Power of *mantras* 107

*Bhakti*—Loving God 108

4. **Gyanayoga** **117**

Ignorance 119

Sin 123

Types of *Karma* 126

Twenty-four Elements 129

*Prakriti Triguna* 130

Attachment 133

Detachment 134

Forgiveness 138

Money 139

Happiness 144

5. **Knowing 'Self' is Knowing God** **161**

Spirituality 161

Knowing 'Self' 165

Knowing God 170

Duality 174

Non-duality 175

Silence 178

Bliss 179

God is Light 181

*Sakshatkar* 182

Awareness 184

Brahman 187

*Samadhi* 190

| | |
|---|---|
| *Moksha* | 191 |
| *Sannyas* | 192 |
| Meditation | 195 |
| *Vairagya* (Aloneness) | 201 |
| Heaven is Within Self | 204 |
| Loneliness is Painful while Aloneness is Bliss | 204 |

ॐ पूर्णमदः पूर्णमिदं पूर्णात् पूर्णमुदच्यते।
पूर्णस्य पूर्णमादाय पूर्णमेवावशिष्यते॥
ॐ शान्तिः शान्तिः शान्तिः॥

# The Philosophy of the *Gita*

'**Bhagvad Gita** *is a pure philosophy of life; not religion.*'

# 1

# Beginning

The basic philosophy of the *Bhagvad Gita* is when Lord Krishna tells Arjuna, "Arjuna, *karmayoga* is better than *sannyasyoga*.

Arjuna, you be a *karmayogi*."

This philosophy of *karmayoga* was relevant then and is relevant now and has a great future. Arjuna asks, "Which of the two—*karmayoga* or *sannyasyoga*—is good?"

Lord Krishna replies, *'The yoga of renunciation of work and the yoga of action are both good for liberation. But of the two, the yoga of action is superior to the yoga of renunciation.'*

This explains that Krishna was against repression (bringing people under control by force). He wanted people to accept life in all its colours. He Himself accepted life unconditionally by not running away from love, war. That is why Krishna's philosophy has great significance today. His philosophy of *karmayoga* will continue to grow with passage of time.

It is easy to understand why a man runs away from the world in search of inner peace, but it is really difficult to accept that one can find peace, happiness and liberation by leading a *grihastha jeevan*. Krishna gave us *karmayoga* to remain unattached and innocent amid relationships and materialism.

Through Krishna's philosophy of *karmayoga*, man has tested his own strength and intelligence, and found that it is possible to perform our duties without attachment, and by surrendering the results to the Supreme Lord. Man can stay untouched with sins by following *karmayoga*, just as the lotus leaf remains untouched by the dirty water in which it grows.

A *karmayogi* believes in living his life here on this earth by performing his deeds and believing in:

*"Karmanyavadhikaraste Ma phaleshukadachana."*

A *karmayogi* refuses to follow those people who renounce life. Lord Krishna believed in living the life of *karma* over *sannyas*. If a *sannyasi* is unable to control his *indriyan* (senses), there is no point in him taking up *sannyas* and live in the Himalayas.

Religious beliefs in renunciation or *sannyas* become meaningless if we are unable to control our desires. A *sannyasi* looking for *moksha* is somewhere beyond this world, while a *karmayogi* can enjoy life while doing *nishkam karma*.

For people to understand *karmayoga* is not simple. After all, we all do our *karmas*, then how is it that we are unable to get the *karmaphal* in the form of happiness, joy and peace. Rather, we suffer from serious illnesses, worries, depression and so on. The problem is we do not understand the actual meaning of *karma*.

When Krishna says *karmayoga*, He means *nishakam karmayoga*, which means doing our deeds, such as looking after our family, children, career, societal duties by taking full responsibilities without expecting anything in return.

Selfless *karma* is a simple but comprehensive way to explain how understanding the true meaning of *karma* can bring happiness in our lives.

*Nishkam karma* results in inner awakening by abandoning ignorance, hatred, anger, desire, attachment, greed and so on. Selfless *karma* can transform our life and enable us to discover our true nature.

*Karma* is one of the inescapable laws of universe. In

*Kaliyuga*, the true meaning of *karma* is rarely understood but the fact is that *karma* is a very deep spiritual philosophy explained in the *Bhagvad Gita* by Krishna when Arjuna was reluctant to perform his duties on the battlefield.

In *Kaliyuga*, the philosophy of selfless *karma* has lost much of its significance as people are drawn towards more materialistic things in life. They are not concerned about the fact that their actions in this life will have an impact, not only in this life, but their next birth too.

We realise the meaning of *karma* when something unfortunate happens which is difficult to explain. But if we are a soul-searching person, we can realise that our past deeds in life have affected our present life. This self-realisation helps us to transform our life in such a way that we consciously tend to avoid bad *karma* as you realise that our negative actions can affect our entire family, our entire surroundings. We realise that nature and natural forces are beyond our control and can cause havoc in our life. We start realising that negative deeds done in previous birth as well as this birth result in sufferings in this life. Similarly, positive, carefully analysed behaviour leads to happiness and joy in our present life.

**This basic philosophy of *karma* is relevant today as it was before. No one can escape *the karmaphal.***

It is beyond my reach and capacity to write in my book the philosophy of *karma*. The way the law of *karma* operates, the way the seed of *karma* develops into a tree, reveal the universal truth of *karma* that affects us. Whether or not we believe in the theory of *karma*, we get affected by it as *karma* is a natural and inescapable law of nature.

***'As you sow, so shall you reap.'***

It means that whatever we are experiencing in this life, we alone are responsible for it. Our *karmas* in the form of our actions are the inevitable consequences. Generally, people blame God for their sufferings. God has nothing to do with our sufferings.

Krishna says:

*'I envy no one, nor am I partial to anyone. I am equal to all. But who all worship me with devotion are in me and I am in them.'*

He has neither attachment for a virtuous man nor hatred for an evil-doer.

There is a system working inside everyone which keeps an account for our actions. These actions, whether good or bad, are the seeds which are sown and when the time comes, these seeds become the trees which bear fruit and we obtain the fruit according to the seeds we have sown. We receive the *karmaphal* according to our good or bad actions. This is the only truth. Nothing else matters. Ego, hate, jealousy, attachment, desires, greed are a few seeds that carry us towards our suffering, disease, unhappiness and dissatisfaction.

It is important to know that *karma* is about learning and not about punishment.

## Our Choice is Our *Karma*

We cannot blame others for our sufferings, our doings. Our free will is our choice. Most of the time we choose a particular path and in order to achieve material gain, we opt for a short cut. By taking this path (short cut) we might achieve materialistic growth but, in the bargain, we head towards a difficult path in our coming life.

*Karma* is the ultimate justice in the form of *karmaphal.* Nothing is overlooked or missed while receiving the *karmaphal.*

Our lives and that of others will be affected if we make the wrong choices. Our past *karmas* had planned our physical life long before our birth. We are destined to meet people and face opportunities as well as obstacles as per our *karma.* How we handle these situations are the result of our free will. Our behaviour, reactions and decisions are the results of our free will. This free will becomes our *karma*, which turns into destiny. We choose our circumstances to plan our lives, while our *karmas* plan our birth in our families. So, we have chosen our birth in that particular family. We can call it destiny. Our good and bad *karmas* plan our destiny—this life as well as our next life. So, growing and learning by correcting our mistakes will take us to a different level, depending on how far we want to progress in *karmayoga.*

*Nishkam karmayoga* is next to godliness. Krishna approves of selfless *karma*. Those who perform *nishkam karma* receive the greatest reward in the form of peace, joy and happiness. Let God handle all our earthly needs if we do our actions properly. He does not favour accumulation of wealth on earth. Trust me it will get spoiled or thieves in the form of near and dear ones will steal it or we may have to pay the doctors for fighting life-threatening diseases. We should accumulate treasure in the form of good deeds and we will get whatever we want in life without putting much effort, because God now begins to reward our selfless deeds. God helps us to accomplish all our desires and materialistic comforts.

Selfless *karmayoga* helps us to become a spiritual person without much effort, making us feel happy, satisfied and righteous. Our decision is very important as to who we want to serve—*God or money* because we cannot serve both. If we cannot give up money, we dare not think about happiness. But selfless *karma* will get us whatever we want in our life.

While selfish *karma* will give us materialistic gains but it will snatch away our happiness. Good deeds take the form of 'getting whatever we want', while bad deeds deprive us of happiness, despite possessing everything under the sun.

## Our *Karma* Today Defines Our Future Tomorrow

Every action has a reaction. We are trapped in the grip of

*karma*, regardless of the circumstances. We cannot run away with wrongdoings. All past actions make their way to return home. We write our own destiny in the form of *karmaphal.*

**What is *karmaphal* and how does it operate?**

**Every action, whether good or bad, is a seed sown inside us.**

A little advancement on the path of selfless *karmayoga* protects us from the fear of bad *karmaphal*. Selfish *karma* is totally materialistic and leads to the cycle of birth and death, while in selfless and detached *karma*, there is no loss of effort, nor is there any fear of contrary results. That is why Krishna gave utmost importance to *karmayoga*.

The *Bhagvad Gita* tells us the definition of good *karma* and bad *karma*. If we experience inner calm, peace, joy, clarity of thoughts and knowing 'self', then it shows that we are on the right path. If we experience illness, turmoil, chaos and unrest inside us, tremendous sufferings and struggle in life then it means that we should look within. Something is not right about our approach towards life. It is not easy for a materialistic person to understand this, but the truth is that we never get something for nothing. There is nobody in this world to help you to search peace because peace has nothing to do with the outer world. It lies within and there is no teacher who can take you to the inner world, where peace and happiness reside. It is our inner world which decides what we have achieved. If money, power, name, fame is our achievement, then it implies that we are aiming towards lust, *kaam vasna*. Then we cannot blame or crib that we are not happy inwardly despite having everything.

We need to accept we are a materialistic person and we crave for people's approval. We want people to praise us whether they are doing it just to please us or out of fear. It is our false ego which makes us think that we can achieve anything and everything. We think 'I' am to be superior to others and that none can match me.

A materialistic person does not mind acquiring money, power, status by harming others. On the other hand, a *karmayogi* is one who performs selfless deeds, is very rooted and stable and cannot be shaken by criticism of a materialist. He is not looking for our approval because he is detached from all materialism. He remains motivated to lead a worthy life. He stays in the world and at same time stays out of it.

Though he is detached, at the same time outer existence must go on. A *karmayogi* firmly rejects the outworldly pressures and others' criticism repeatedly. He does not give up his belief that aim is to know the 'self'. His strong will and *nishkam karma* bear fruit. He remains private while inwardly he is working at full swing. He remains in the world but detached and isolated at the same time. This is like performing the balancing act.

For a materialistic person life is very difficult as he limits himself to money, power, lust, *kaam vaasna.*

Though it is difficult to come out of materialism but it cannot be considered impossible.

As Krishna says:

*'One who is able to withdraw his five senses from the sense objects just as the tortoise draws its limbs within its shell, then his mind becomes stable.'*

Most people are servants of the senses, the *indriya.*

If we want happiness in life, we have to be strong enough to control our desires. Unless we are able to follow do's and dont's, it is not possible to lead a happy, joyous and peaceful life.

In the materialistic world, a *karmayogi* can lead a life of renunciation while leading a perfect *grihastha jeevan.* Those, who know the inner happiness, inner self can think and live in an ordinary way. They appear normal, behave normally because they maintain a perfect balance between the outer and inner worlds. While a greedy, selfish *sannyasi*, no matter how secluded a life he may be leading in the Himalayas, he will not be able to lead a life of renunciation.

Krishna says:

*'One, who refrains the senses but whose mind is thinking of the objects of enjoyment all the time, is a hypocrite.'*

For enjoyment of senses, one can act in any capacity. One can make a show of being a yogi, but if one has no control over his senses, he is deceiving people. His being a *sannyasi* has no value.

That is the reason Lord Krishna prefers a *grihastha jeevan* over *sannyas.*

In *grihastha jeevan,* while doing our household chores, performing our duties for our family, relatives, career and society, we can stay active outwardly and maintain our inner search. By doing *nishkam karma,* we can become the maker of our own destiny.

Selfish *karma* is ongoing, never ending.

*Karma* for material world means forcing ourselves to do the same *karma* again and again. We become a slave of our desires that lead to actions, which lead to more desires. Selfish *karma* means always wanting more and this will not take us anywhere. When we do selfless *karma,* we no longer chase and run after materialistic things, while materialistic *karma* forces us to do the same action again and again. This process is never ending and you are liable to get bored at some stage and at the end of this material chase, we end up emptyhanded.

*'Duvidha mei dono gaye, maya mili na Rama.'*

No point in living in a dream world because on waking up, we will realise that we were chasing a *mrigtrishna*, an illusion. Eventually we come to realise that our material desires were leading us to the wrong path. *Nishkam karma* leads us towards the spiritual path without putting in any efforts as we are not running after an illusion.

## Debts must be Paid

*'Paying debts does not mean paying in material form.'*

If we don't pay our debts in this life, we carry these debts to another life. Performing our selfless duties, as parents, children, relatives, friends help us to lead a debt-free life, which in turn, leads to a peaceful journey at the later stage of our life. It makes our old age very comfortable without putting in much effort. *Karmayoga* is a path where nothing is missed or overlooked. This path gives us ultimate justice.

If we have learned our lessons, understood the reasons for our sufferings due to wrong actions, we will find that our sufferings are less. Even if the debts are not fully paid, we experience some respite which encourages us to become absolutely debt-free, so that we can enjoy a peaceful and happy life ahead.

## *Karma* is to Learn from Our Wrongdoings

In this birth, we are here to learn that our life-slate should be kept clean. This life has to be taken as an opportunity to wipe the slate and make it debt-free. If we think it is difficult, then we are wrong. The mud which makes us dirty is the same mud that cleanses our utensils. Similarly the 'attached *karma*' makes our life full of sufferings while 'detached *karma*' makes it liberated. We can clean our dirt in the form of attachment, desires, *mohmaya* by doing *nishkam karma.*

The main secret, the *rahasyamayi sutra* of *Bhagvad Gita* is: *Karmanyavadhi karaste Ma phaleshukadachana.*

'We have the right to perform our duties without being attached to the results.'

One who is attached to the result of his work is also the cause of *karma,* which means *bandhan,* the cause of bondage. We must perform our deeds as a matter of duty without attachment to the result.

*Karma* is an opportunity to amend our wrongdoings in this birth so that we can make up to those we may have wronged or hurt in the past.

*Karma* is to practice love and forgiveness and pay our karmic debts. We are daily redefining ourselves. If love and hatred, trust and suspicion are contradictory in our mind, then we must be careful as these may appear insignificant, but create a 'seed'. Our actions, thoughts and their consequences are influenced by tiny little factors throughout our lives. It is not easy to understand how *karma* operates. Our perception of external events and the way we handle these situations affects our *karma*. This simple thing to understand does not require technology. It is not a rocket science to know that nothing right will happen in our life if we do wrong things. Considering ourself to be a good human being is fine. We may be well respected in the society and this too is fine. We may have a position in society and this is fine. But unless we achieve all these things through the right means and have not harmed anybody, we cannot stay calm and peaceful. Happiness will never come to us.

Inner happiness accepts only *nishkam karma*, not money, power, status, etc. Life does not work the way we like. It works, only if we follow the do's and don'ts in life.

## The *Karmic* Chain

Human life depends on the will of a person to escape from the *karmic* chain.

Man should not be a slave of his past *karmas*. *Karmas* should not make us into puppets. Man should come up with strong will power and determination to be free from every limitation. Good and bad actions are measured and accordingly rewards and punishments are given.

Past-life *karmas* have given us an abnormal life. We are born as handicapped, retarded, OBC or LGBT. It requires serious introspection to learn from this and try to introspect on our own. Instead of looking for mercy, or being bitter towards society for treating us differently, or to indulge in self-pity by asking 'why me' or 'what wrong have I done', we must learn from this and try to change our *karma*. We should understand that our past-life *karma* has given us an abnormal life. Instead of taking several births as retarded or physically impaired, we ought to learn from our current life only, so that in our next birth, we have a normal and fulfilling life.

**To achieve this, breaking of the *karmic* chain is the only solution.**

Why should we suffer? Once we were to introspect and do soul searching, we will notice our will power arise in a bid to escape from this *karmic* chain. None other than us are responsible for the causes. Now we want to undo what was done in the past. Knowing that past *karmic* seeds are the reasons for our unhappy and abnormal life, we should not nurture the seeds of destructive tendencies by resorting to fresh evil *karmas*. We must not allow our past seeds to sprout; rather, use our present life to break the *karmic* chain by doing conscious efforts to lead a sin-free life. We can engage in definite, step-by-step procedures by disciplining ourselves and taking nothing for granted. There are many tried and tested series of spiritual exercises, prayers, yoga and meditation described by our ancient *rishis* and sages.

Since we have decided that in this birth only we would like to strengthen our abilities by *nishkam karma*, this growing awareness that we can awaken our inner dormant powers will increase the chances of our success. At this point, we will feel more comfortable and familiar with ourself.

Although true growth is an inner process and every

human being is capable of awakening his or her inner powers, but if we want, we can seek help to learn the techniques and means to do *kriya*, meditation and yoga while the rest has to be done on our own.

**We must not surrender ourself to anyone other than God.**

The *guru* can be important to us only if he helps to make us understand that there is much more to our lives than we are usually aware of.

The theory of *nishkam karmayoga* described by Lord Krishna is the only successful method of breaking the *karmic* chain. In *kaliyuga*, hardly any *guru* is promoting this philosophy. There are hardly any *gurus* who feel responsible enough to show and teach their disciples the divine path of *nishkam karmayoga.* We have to be lucky enough to find a true *guru*. We need to understand the fact that *gurus* cannot be our saviour; God alone is our saviour and a great healer, but in *kaliyuga*, *gurus* promote themselves and not God. They promote the other methods but never teach *karmayoga.* No *guru* can introduce us to ourself. We have to do it by ourselves as we have the ultimate power to know the 'self' lying dormant inside us. On awakening this power by performing *nishkam karma*, we will notice that spirituality exists within us and not outside us.

In *kaliyuga*, why is it that most people are unable to fathom their own self? This is because they are busy running after the *gurus* and have no time to introspect themselves. Stop wasting time. Spend that time on praying, meditating at home. Trust me, *bhakti* and *nishkam karma* will stop us from taking any wrong action. We will not need any *guru*. God Himself will become our *guru*. He will show us the right path and stop us from taking any wrong decision. He will provide us with all the comforts without us asking for anything. He will plan our present and future. We will be surprised to receive His unlimited rewards in the form of good life, good health, peace and joy. We must surrender ourself completely, have faith in Him and He will not disappoint us.

Krishna says:

*'O son of Kunti, declare it boldly that my devotee never perishes.'*

*He quickly becomes joyous and attains lasting peace.*

We all accumulate good and bad *karmas*, not only in this life, but in previous births too. If we want to undo our negative *karma*, there are ways in which we can clean our negative *karmas* and break the *karmic* chain.

## Ways to Break the *Karmic* Chain

When we face our child's death, the trauma that we go through, the mental agony we face, is terrible. At that point we come to realise that something has gone wrong, that we have done some wrong *karma*, either in this life or our previous life. We get completely shattered. At this traumatic stage, if we truly want to come out of it, God shows us the way. We do not want to face this tragedy again in our life. We have understood by now that there is some past *karmic* connection and we want to break this *karmic* chain.

Similarly, when we come across handicapped and mentally-retarded people in our life, we see that their families have to suffer along with them. We notice that many people have all the best possible things in their lives. They have name, fame, money and power, but are unable to lead a normal life. There are many categories in society, where, instead of emerging out of this situation through hard work and dedication, they indulge in self-pity and seek mercy in the form of grants and job reservation. They don't realise that they are in this situation because of their past *karmas*. We cannot change this birth but surely we can change our next birth by leading more 'aware' of life.

Our awareness reveals the truth of *karma* by itself. This awareness is an experience which we cannot learn from rituals or a *guru* or a teacher.

To achieve this awareness, in the *Bhagvad Gita*, Lord Krishna specifies three ways:

1. *Gyanayoga*
2. *Karmayoga*
3. *Bhaktiyoga*

By practicing any one of them, we can reach the path of 'awareness', which means *gyana*. *Gyana* means doing *nishkam karma, yoga* and *bhakti*.

□

# Karmayoga

'Nishkam karma *is the only one which is perfectly pure and devoid of any* karmaphal.'

# Karmayoga

'**T***he law of* **karma** *is basically the law of cause and effect.*'

*Karma* is derived from the Sanskrit word, *kri,* which means 'to do'. *Karma* means 'action', 'work' or 'deed'. To be living in the physical world, doing our deeds, such as looking after our family, children, career, societal duties, by taking on full responsibilities, is *karma*. *Karma* is action, action as the will to do something. The fact that every action creates an effect, in that sense it is the force behind all the changes and this, whether we realise it or not, is the big deal.

Doing things is inherent to man's very nature.

Krishna says:

*'No one can ever remain inactive even for a moment without doing any deed.'*

*Karma* is a word that comes up a lot in day-to-day life and this is a good reason for us getting drawn to this intriguing subject. The word *karma* fascinates us; it mystifies us. The *karma* philosophy is not law; it is the very nature of life. But it is complex; it is not so simple to be understood. When Lord Krishna talked about *karmayoga* while giving Arjuna '*Gita*'s *gyana*, it became a universal definition. Though man has gone far away from the ancient law of *karma*, but whether we like it or not, it still remains relevant; more relevant in this *kaliyuga*.

No one can escape one's *karmaphal.* The *karma* theory is that whether we do good or bad; it registers itself automatically. *Karma*—that which goes against the law of nature, which goes against ourselves—is a crime, a bad *karma.*

How can we know what is a crime? Whenever we do anything against the law of nature, it records in our subconsciousness. It records in such a way that it starts making us suffer from a feeling of guilt. We start feeling unworthy and this causes hurt and pain inside us. If we do bad *karma,* a feeling of being below human, a feeling of inferiority, overcomes us. If we cheat somebody, it registers deep inside us. Unconsciously we know that we have been dishonest and we cannot relax. We become tense and this tension creates tension among the people around us. *Karma* has an effect on man's character and personality and if we are conscious of it, it becomes a great challenge which we need to handle.

Every crime against one's own nature, everyone without exception, records itself in the book of inner conscious. There are no books which God keeps. We are the book! Whatsoever we are, whatsoever we do, is constantly being monitored and registered. Not that there is somebody noting it down; it is a natural phenomenon. There is no one keeping a record of our *karma*; we alone are masters of our *karmas. Karma* is that if we do something wrong which we are ashamed of, it registers to our discredit. And if we do something good, it registers to our credit. We can observe it; we can watch it. The law of *karma* is not some philosophy; it is simply a theory which explains the truth inside our very being. The net result is that either we respect ourselves or we despise and feel worthless. For every moment, every action we perform, we create for ourselves either a grace or a disgrace. This is the result of *karma*. None can avoid it; none can cheat or manipulate it because it is impossible.

In today's world, man takes it for granted and because of his ego, he thinks that it is he who does everything and feels, '*I am the doer of all activities and nobody is above me.*' But the fact, according to Lord Krishna, in the *Gita* is: "All actions are being performed by the modes of *prakriti* (nature)." The qualities we have taken from *trigunas* are *sattva, rajasa* and *tamasa* which will incite us to take action because we are under the influence of *prakriti*. These three forces are present in all of us. In all of creation, that is, animals, plants and human beings, we find more or less manifestations of all these three *gunas*. *Karmayoga* entails dealing with these three factors, as no one can escape from doing one's *nitya karma*. Nature's law compels us, be it willingly or unwillingly, to act. Man is just an entity in his ordinary capacity and he is just a puppet in the hands of the *trigunas*.

According to Patanjali:

'Our past thoughts and actions leave an impression on our subconscious mind. These impressions, known as *samskaras*, are stored in our subconscious memory which manifest as our mental habits and tendencies. And these mental habits determine our character. Our *samskaras* are an expression of our past *karma* and they also help to determine the way we will act in future. Each of us carries *samskaras* of past thoughts and actions. These *samskaras* can create patterns in the field of our thought process and our consciousness. There are negative *karmas* in every area of life. Changing negative *karma* involves working through our attitude and behaviour, while ethical behaviour aligns us with positive forces in the universe. We can follow helpful skills, such as yoga, meditation and consuming *satvic* food and practicing *satvic* behaviour.

Change in our *karma* includes changing the way we live our day-to-day life. This implies making small choices to shift out of patterns that may be keeping old *karmas* in place. By changing our way of doing things, we can create new *samskaras* and hence, new *karmic* effects.

When we want to change our life, it is wise to begin by looking into our habitual thought patterns and thought processes. We can start by making choices that allow us to break from the old cycle of *karmic* chain. This means beginning by setting a strong intention to make a shift in our thinking or behaviour and then analysing what steps we can take to implement that shift. Our past thoughts and actions have enormous power in our present to influence our life in future.

'Our *karma* today defines our future tomorrow.' There are three kinds of *karma*:

1. *Sanchita karma*
2. *Prarabdha karma*
3. *Kriyamana karma*

*Sanchita karma*

All actions, good or bad, from one's past life follow through to the next life. *Sanchita* is all the accumulated *karmas* of the past.

*Prarabdha karma*

*Prarabdha* is that portion of the past *karma*, which is responsible for the present body. The portion of *Sanchita karma* which influences human life in the present incarnation is called *prarabdha*. It is ripe for reaping. It cannot be avoided or changed. We pay our past debts.

*Kriyamana karma*

*Kriyamana* is that *karma* which is now being readied for the future. It is also called *agami* or *vartamana*.

According to the theory of *karma*, what happens to a person, happens because he or she must have caused it with his or her own actions.

Life is very precious, so there is no reason to waste it. Our *karmas* plan our present life as well as our next life. We must take full responsibility for this.

*Karma* is a belief that whatever we do will come back to us, either in this life or in the next. Belief in the *karma* theory means believing in *cause* and *effect*, that is, nothing happens on its own. *Karma* is not itself a reward or punishment, but the law of nature that results in consequences.

So, while doing *karma*, we have to be consciously very careful because once we have performed a deed, or taken an action, we cannot take it back. The *karma* gets created and we will definitely experience the effects in future.

We cannot make God responsible for our miseries. God is not punishing us for our bad deeds or rewarding us for the good ones. The actions themselves decide what we experience.

When we say bad luck to a suffering person, it has nothing to do with *luck*; it may be indeed his *karmas*. When we think about it and realise that everyone has suffered some misfortune as also some good things in their lives, it means that this is the nature of their *karma*.

In today's world, everyone is running after material gain, be it by hook or by crook. They believe, happiness means possessing wealth. We desire to have a nice home, a satisfying career, children, expensive possessions and so on. When we achieve them, we crave for more to keep ourselves happy. But do these things make us happy? No! Because we achieve this at the cost of our peace of mind and happiness. And if our desires remain unfulfilled, we feel dissatisfied.

*'Fulfilment of our desires at any cost does not bring us real and lasting happiness.'*

This does not mean that it is wrong to possess nice things. If they come our way without causing any harm, then we should certainly enjoy them.

In life we see that all the honest people are losers and immoral people are gainers. The cunning and clever become powerful and the simple and straightforward get crushed. We may call it fate and justify to ourself by saying that we will have a better fate in our future life and the cunning and dishonest will have a bitter fate in his future life. This is a beautiful consolation but it is not true.

The belief in fate is simply a consolation because we cannot accept our failure as a failure. Our failure calls for honest soul-searching. If we do so, we will know the real reason for our failure. Maybe our efforts were not selfless.

The fact is that the cunning man succeeds because of his dishonesty, not because of his fate.

He succeeds because he does not care what kind of means and ways he adopts to win. It is up to us to decide what ways we want to adopt. Fate is not written; we write our own fate. If we live our life by honest means, God accepts it. God helps us to abide by our path, even after we face hurdles while leading a truthful and honest life.

It is our personal contact with reality which makes you completely at ease and we feel there is a great harmony in life.

At this stage, success of a dishonest and cunning person becomes immaterial to us. We are so comfortable with our own self that we are not jealous of other people's money, power or status because we know that they have earned it through wrong and unjust means. It does not bother us that somebody is rich or the other person is poor, or that somebody is successful and the other is not.

When people face some crisis in life, like a serious illness or irreparable damage or loss, their attitude towards life undergoes a change. If we are wise, we will take it as a warning and will do self– analysis as analysing will help and the real change would occur. Our inner voice will tell us what is wrong.

In my case, when I lost my daughter Neha, I realised that due to my past *karmas* I had faced this situation. I wanted to break my *karmic* chain. I wanted to come out of depression. I chose the *bhakti marg* to break the *karmic* chain.

Trust me, God helped me completely. He was there for me at every stage in life.

But, if we are materially attached, our *indriyas* (senses) get contaminated with selfishness and self-centredness. We are ready to suffer but not ready to improve our ways. If we do not listen to our inner voice and are not ready to mend our ways, then we have to prepare ourselves to face disaster and destruction in our life.

We do not need technology to be happy and contented in life. If we need well-being, we need to change our ways in life completely. Unless we institute these changes, nothing right is going to happen in our life.

Happiness, peace and joy accept only *nishkam karma*, not money, power, ego, etc. Life does not work for us if we don't take on the responsibility for our materialistic ways in life.

'*Real happiness comes when we eliminate selfish or attached karmas.*'

Human life is full of sorrows until we realise that the selfish *karma* is the main reason responsible for it. Our life depends on our will to escape the bad *karmas*. We can overcome any limitations, because we create it by our own wrong deeds in the first place. If we think it is difficult and not possible, then we are wrong.

Krishna says:

'*The* indriyas *(senses) are greater than the body, but the mind is higher than the senses. Intelligence is still higher than the mind and the soul is even greater and higher than the intellect.*'

The hierarchy of bodily functions described here by Lord Krishna ultimately leads to the supremacy of soul, which means God realisation.

If the soul is directly engaged to God, then naturally all other subordinate *indriyas*, namely, intelligence, mind and senses, will be automatically engaged directly with the

Supreme. At this stage, there is no possibility of the senses becoming engaged in other ways. When we have tasted the higher transcendental force, there is no chance of us being engaged in the lower propensities.

Materialism and egoistic desires are like a magnet which attracts iron fillings of attached *karma*. And this attached *karma* is the main cause of our sufferings. Today, we are trapped in an endless cycle of desires and dissatisfaction.

To understand the simple laws of *karma*, their causes and effects we must know that every action, however tiny or insignificant, creates a seed. So, every action is like sowing a seed inside us. It grows and turns into a field of fruits.

Krishna explains: *'This body is called the field—the field of activity, deed and action. When we sow a seed in the field or a farm, it develops into crop. This crop multiplies and when the right time comes, we cut the crop or harvest it from the field.'*

Similarly, our body is like a field in which the crop of our actions, deeds and activities flourishes. This action or deed in our body grows day by day. One *karma* gives birth to another *karma*. When the time comes, the impact and results of our action and deed are ready. We start experiencing the results of our *karma*. This is the law of nature *(prakriti)* and nobody can change this law.

This body is the field of activity and is composed of material nature. Whatever one is supposed to do, either for happiness or sorrow, one is forced to do because of the bodily constitution. This body is given according to one's past desires. To fulfil desires, one is given the body with which one acts accordingly. Because of the desires, one faces difficult circumstances, which are meant to be suffered or enjoyed. In our body field, *karma* seeds flourish and eventually the results of our actions are unavoidable. Our actions and their consequences are influenced by these insignificant factors throughout our entire lives.

It is not easy to understand how *karma* operates in today's world. In *kaliyuga,* people seek happiness by achieving money, power, name and fame without realising that everything is temporary. So, even if we create the cause to be happy, the resulting happiness cannot last forever. Sooner or later our deeds are unable to impart happiness and we will then experience sufferings.

In today's world, *karma* means always wanting more of what won't get us anywhere. *Karma* is an infinite and ongoing process, but, doing deeds thoughtfully and carefully release us from the *karmic* influences.

The material world forces us to repeat the same *karma* again and again. Our life journey is not a dream or a chase. Every action has a consequence. Every man, by his thoughts and deeds becomes in-charge and can change his destiny. Deeds and actions which he took wisely or unwisely, intentionally or unintentionally, return to him in the form of *karmaphal,* which is impossible to stop. At this stage, every crime is punished and every good action is rewarded. We receive a reward in the form of good or bad results.

*Good results:* Inner peace, joy, clarity of thoughts.

We also receive good physical awards in the form of food, clothing, shelter, a loving family and good health.

*Bad results:* Illness, disease, unhappiness, chaotic thoughts.

Also bad physical results are obtained in the form of being left alone and abandoned or suffering.

There is no other way to avoid bad *karma* but to continue doing our karmas consciously. It means taking full responsibility. If we keep on deserting our ordinary responsibilities, we will face misfortune.

It takes a great deal of growing up before one lives with the continuous experience of good and bad, love and hate, dark and light. If we want to have a happy and peaceful life, we should resolve the conflicts, such as love and anger, peace and violence. If we are in misery, it is because of our own actions and if we are happy, it is because of our own deeds.

*A person's free will or choice made in a particular karmic situation is the cause of his sufferings or happiness. His choice and free will become the moulder of his destiny.*

It is important to understand that *karma* operates in a complex way over many lifetimes. We create *karma* through our body, speech and mind. The law of *karma* states that we must have acted at some point in a way to cause our own sufferings.

Free will is how we act and reach at each moment in response to the situation, ability to think and plan. We have a choice in terms of how we handle the difficult *karmic* situations in life. Our choice of *karmic* action can be our strength or weakness.

*'Acceptance of weakness is a great strength.'*

Choose to address the cause of the problem.

## *Karmic* Seeds

***'As we sow, so shall we reap.'***

The law of *karma*, as stated by Lord Krishna, relates to action and reaction, cause and effect, sowing and reaping. What goes around, comes around.

Every *karma* is a seed. Seeds in the form of *karma* mean taking personal responsibility for our own actions.

The person who has happiness, health and success, creates the seeds for a pleasant life by performing detached *karma* in previous life as well as in present life. Those who suffer from poverty, illness, misfortune, create the seeds and causes of their unpleasant experiences by committing bad deeds in this life as well as in previous life. This makes one thing very clear—that we ourselves are responsible for whatever occurs in our lives.

We are trapped in the cycle of *karmaphal*, not only in this birth, but in the next birth too. Our choice is the seed which is sown inside us and which grows into a tree, producing innumerable fruits.

The reason for our suffering is that our bad *karmic* seeds have sprouted either of this life or past life. Our further evil action will water our past *karmic* seeds. We ought to avoid watering our past *karmic* seed with negative *karmas,* otherwise the seed will turn into a field with a flourishing crop. We should not nurture the past *karmic* seeds by repeating the same mistakes again in this birth.

*'Do not water the past karmic seeds with your evil deeds.'*

The moment our *karmic* action begins, a seed is sown inside us. If our actions are ego-oriented, they are negative seeds. This means unhappiness and miseries.

The *Gita* tells us about the negative seeds caused by our actions and behaviour.

*'By avoiding the following negative attitudes and behaviour, we can sow the seeds of positivity in our life.'*

## Negative (Dark) Seeds

**Ego:** The seed of ego came into this world with us. Ego is the result of *karma.* It is the person's sense of self-esteem or self-importance. Self- centredness and false pride constitute ego. Someone's ego is their sense of their own worth. If someone has a large ego, he thinks himself very important and valuable.

Lord Krishna tells Arjuna:

*'Our ego is the reason for our dilemmas or confusion.'*

There is a fundamental difference between *'real'* ego and *'false'* ego. Real ego is an essence in our personality that makes us aware and conscious of the reality. False ego is a false identity, which one creates to be the most important and significant person of all time. The *worst,* false ego blinds one from doing honest introspection and admittance.

False egocentric people are busy pointing fingers at others' behaviour rather than looking at themselves. False ego fancies itself as more 'advanced' than it actually is.

The *Bhagvad Gita's* solution to handle false ego is introspection and self- knowledge.

For this we need courage and humility. The more we practice self-awareness, the more we can realise that it is not others who are good or evil, rather it is our own ego-centric judgements.

It is not bad to have ego but we should know how to handle it. Ego gives us strength though the end result is painful because ego (*Ahankar)* believes in acquiring more and more.

Ego is insatiable. Though we have everything at the present stage, but we fear suffering the loss of what we have. This fear of loss closes our mind. We become unwilling to take reasonable risks to try out something new. Because of this fear, our instincts stop working. The fear of loss makes us empty inside, leading to the path of chaos in life and forcing us to get whatever we want even at the cost of ignoring other people's needs.

Ego is one of the most misunderstood term. Ego is identical to 'self'. *Aham* equates with Brahman Himself (*aham atman, aham Brahmasmi*). But when this ego becomes *ahankar* then the person becomes arrogant and develops false sense of identity, accepting it as true.

False ego is a feeling of false perception of oneself, that is, being special, a separate being and different from others.

It manifests as pride, arrogance, selfishness, self centredness, aggression, competitiveness, judgement, opinions, criticism, fear, sufferings, anxiety, anger, stress and so on. It happens when a person is over-proud and conceited.

Any suffering we experience, any discomfort and disturbance in life, is due to ego, which makes us believe that we are the doers of our actions and responsible for them.

Ego is very shallow because shallowness is in the nature of ego. The egoist, who does not know much, thinks he knows. The entire world is suffering from the disease of 'ego' and that is why everyone is facing unhappiness.

Lord Krishna personifies the universal Self with the purest and indistinguishable ego, whereas Arjuna symbolises limited self. Arjuna suffers because of his limited knowledge about his body rather than his soul.

There are two aspects to us—one is the *real* us and the other is the *projected* us. The world knows us by the *projected* us. It does not know the *real* us because it is hidden under the mask of our projected personality. Here 'ego' signifies identity. We should give up the false identification with the body.

The sense of *I am* is ego, but when the sense of *'I am'* is applied to this false body, it becomes false ego, like for example, 'I have achieved so much', 'I am superior to others, 'no one is close to me', 'I am the best', 'I am the greatest in the world'. This becomes *ahankar,* which is the worst enemy of our happiness.

We become self-centred, suffer from false pride, ego, etc. which prevent us from being in the real form. An egoistic person can never enjoy peace and happiness. We are surrounded by our own self, money, house, family, children and this *ahankar* prevents us from seeing ourself beyond it. But our ego becomes powerless when we are faced with a bigger ego. We feel shallow in front of that person. This traps us in the cycle of miseries and sufferings, physically and mentally.

Ego-based actions are 'material' in nature. These actions teach us 'mine' and 'not mine'. When the sense of self is applied to reality, that becomes real ego. When one understands that he is not his body and is soul, he becomes his real ego.

Control of ego is therefore important to experience peace of mind. The one who has control over his ego can become aware of the ego and makes it take a back seat, allowing the 'self' to become the centre of one's life. This is the state of egolessness as well as the pure state of spiritual awareness. In that state a *karmayogi* performs desireless actions without struggles in life. The ego is a barrier which prevents us from seeing the truth about ourself. This sense of 'I am', of self, of 'I am Brahman', 'I am soul', becomes real ego. Real ego makes space for *bhakti* inside us. *Bhakti* means one who has made his false ego, *ahankar*, to bow down. Worship means destroying one's ego. As soon as 'I', 'my', 'me' disappear, God appears. Man is full of ego. Until he drops his ego, he cannot understand God. We must remove our ego to make space for God.

God is beyond self-expression and an individual acknowledgement of the *ahankaris*. They feel that they have the right to decide on God and the universe. They give themselves the right to their personal interpretation of God and the world. Such arrogant *ahankaris* do not pay attention to the truth because they are obsessed with their name, wealth and status. God is beyond such materialism.

When we remove all false ego, then there is spiritual growth. The ego moves from an isolated, helpless state to a 'realisation' that there is a difference between external happiness in the form of materialism and internal happiness in the form of peace, calmness. We realise that the source of happiness is due to our internal power. We don't run after the outer source as the real source is in us, our self. Until we free ourself from pretentions, we cannot understand the external truth or eternal happiness. We ought not to surrender to the common fate but make ourself special by dropping our ego.

We need not think too much about how we can function and survive without ego and stop worrying about what people will think about us. Constant worries, analysis and thoughts prevent our ego from accepting the truth and prevent us from getting rid of our habitual *ahankar*. Our assumptions, preconceived notions, bias ideas, prejudices keep coming in our way. We must control these to save ourselves from total destruction.

It is hard work to stay out of these, but not difficult. We have to eliminate self-centredness and false pride while dropping 'I', 'my', 'me', which are an integral part of our everyday routine.

If we gradually decrease our concern about functioning and fitting into our social world and worrying about what other people would think about 'me', then we can slowly begin to build our happiness.

Ego can never be removed by force. It has to go by itself by understanding its limitations and what obstacles it can create. Ego is hunger for power, pleasure, money, sex; it is insatiable. We have everything but still we are not happy. We want more and we don't mind getting what we desire at the cost of harming others. In this process, the *ahankari* goes too far. Here comes the stage to prevent an egoist from proceeding further; instead here comes God.

To prevent this, we have God, an omnipotent judge who threatens even the most powerful if he goes too far.

That is the world beyond 'I', 'my', 'me'. How can we see that world? How can we see things as they really exist, if our egos are constantly coming in the way?

We can see the beautiful world if we drop our ego and desist from making our need, our desire, our pleasure our priority!!

This is difficult but not impossible.

The journey is tough and long, but well worth it.

**Anger:** *Anger is the defence of ego, defence against fear.'* Anger is a useless emotion as it arises from non-fulfilment of desires, be they good or bad. We get angry because we have not fulfilled our. expectations and fear being humiliated or embarrassed, or fear loss and loss of face.

If we are weak, vulnerable to overcome this, to show

ourselves as superior when we are not, we take the refuge of 'getting angry'. It works as a protective coating for a weak and vulnerable person.

Anger works as a dangerous tool to protect us from the fear of embarrassment or the fear of being feel small or mocked in society. It makes us angry. Instead of making ourself confident and sensible, we become angry, enraged and furious. We don't want to control our anger through anger management as our ego prevents us from doing this. Our ego tells us, "You are correct; the other person is wrong."

Anger is a defence against fear of not getting our way, which leads to violent behaviour and it can break relationships. It can destroy love and compassion.

According to Lord Krishna:

*'Anger or* krodha *arises from unfulfilled desires.'*

Krishna says:

***'Anger can destroy everything on this planet. Anger makes a man violent and he cannot understand others' pain and feelings. Anger blocks the ability to love and respect; that is why a man with anger cannot love. Therefore he cannot attain God.'***

Anger is the manifestation of ignorance. Anger arises when someone puts obstacles in the path of our desires, making us think that it will bring pleasure to us. That obstacle is the cause of our anger.

Anger cannot disappear if the desire is there. So, if we are able to control our desires, then we will be able to shun *krodha.*

Violent behaviour can turn us into an animal, though for a short period. But it can be very destructive for our body and soul.

As soon as anger arises, the angry man is left in the darkness of delusion, without a guide and does not remember what he is supposed to do as loss of memory follows delusion. The angry man forgets what he was and how he should behave. Reasonable thoughts find no means of expression in an angry person; reasonable words have no effect on an angry man.

If someone tends to get angry easily only with spouse, this can be seen as a *karmic* consequence. If our anger is an outburst of uncontrolled emotions due to frustration, then it is very *karmic* and entangling. How can we not be loving and compassionate? How can we not control anger if we love?

No one can control us; we are in control. Then anger is not getting our way.

Anger management is one of the skills we can acquire in order to avoid repetitions of violence in life. Consider anger like an enemy, who is to be fought within ourselves.

Being spiritual along with anger management, we can tackle the most serious problems on Earth. Self-control and anger management give inner calmness. In this state of mind, one is able to experience eternal peace.

We need to turn our anger into a tool, to actually do things in a very effective way. Then it becomes an asset for us, Like Hanuman had done in Lanka, that 'anger' was an expression of love and *bhakti* for Lord Rama.

We have to possess inner spiritual strength in order to use it for that purpose.

*'Anger can be an expression of love and so, can be the determination to control anger'.*

**Greed:** *'Where greed arrives, happiness departs.'* A selfish desire for something beyond one's needs is greed. Intense and selfish desire for something, especially wealth, power or food is greed. Typically, greed is associated with the wealth or power. Greed usually describes someone who cannot have enough of anything and will never be content with what he has, despite the amount.

Greed is a state of mind, even though it is treated through

material and physical meaning outside things. Greed destroys peace of mind.

Lord Krishna says:

*'Contentment is peace; he who is satisfied with what I have given to him will always be in a happy state of mind.'*

So, greed actually disturbs the balance of mind and soul, forcing man to crave for more and more and driving him towards material pleasures. He is no longer living in a spiritual world.

The purpose of greed and any actions associated with it, is possibly to deprive others of the potential means of survival and comfort, or future opportunities or obstruct them through tyrannical treatment.

Greed or being a greedy person is not just a character trait; it is also one's relationship with people and life. A greedy person sees others as a potential catch.

Their mentality is that of a predator, which is always calculating how to use others. A greedy person always competes with others in owning things that he considers as his natural belongings—something that he should have, but accidentally do not. Greed is a *bottomless pit* which exhausts the person in an endless effort to satisfy the need without ever acquiring satisfaction.

Greed always finds an endless field of conquest and leaves the man endlessly dissatisfied.

A greedy person is someone who is not able to or is not willing to control himself. His restlessness of heart craves for power and possession. He is not willing to control himself and wants everything he likes or finds interesting at the moment. Greed means the desire for multiplication of material things. We have one lakh rupees but want ten lakhs; we have one house, but want another house and so on. This greed is multiplication of things. Greed means the desire to get more and more pleasure out of materialistic things.

Greed is a sin against God, just as all mortal sins are. There is sufficiency in the world for man's needs, but not for man's greed, as greed is an insatiable longing for wealth, status and power.

If our greed is a desire to acquire knowledge, it will take us towards wisdom, which will lead to an upward surge of mankind.

**Lust:** Lust is *intense desire* or *longing* for an object, or circumstance that fulfills the emotion. Lust can take any form, such as the lust for sexuality, love, money or power.

Lust is merely for sense enjoyment and when people have indulged in prolonged lustful activities, they lose out on the real purpose of their lives.

Lust is the greatest enemy of the living being and it is lust which makes a person to remain attached to the material world. It is difficult for a lusty person to return to the non-material world.

Sexual desire is a reality; but when it crosses a level, where one forgets the difference between right and wrong, is punishable.

Lust is *kama.* We have misunderstood the word *kama* in general. *Kama* is a strong attraction towards something and it pulls us towards attachment (*bandhan*).

Lust is *vasna* within us due to our past attractions which leave its traces as lust within us. Lust stays in the body, but is given vent through the senses.

The *Bhagvad Gita* mentions precisely that lustful sexual desires are a constant enemy because they are capable of distracting even the most wisest of persons. There is nothing wrong with lust until one seriously abuses himself because of lust. Anyone who is obsessed with lust is already in hell.

Lust cannot be satisfied by any amount of sense enjoyment, just as fire is never extinguished by a constant supply of fuel.

In this material world, the centre of all activities is sex

and thus this material world is described as 'shackles of sex life'. It is lust only which keeps the living entity confined to the material world.

Lord Krishna says:

*'It is lust only, Arjuna, which is born of contact with the material mode of passion. It is insatiable and grossly wicked. Take this as the enemy in this case.'*

It is lust only which induces the pure living entity to remain entangled in materialism. A human being is originally spiritual, pure and free from all materialism. By nature, he is not subject to sins of the material world, like 'lust' and 'anger'.

A living entity is born with different degrees of lust. Even the wise entity's pure consciousness gets attacked by his eternal enemy in the form of lust, which is never satisfied and which burns like fire.

Lust is a constant enemy of the wise, like a raging fire which can never be satisfied.

This lust is a symbol of ignorance by which the living entity is kept within the material world. When one enjoys sense gratification and gets some feeling of happiness, this so-called feeling of happiness is the ultimate enemy of the sense-enjoyer.

If someone's lust is interrupted, he gets angry and starts hating. Hatred in the world today is due not out of love, but out of lust. A person who indulges in lust becomes manipulative and cunning.

Lust or *vasna* is an animal instinct. It stays in the body, but is given vent through the senses. *Kama, vasna*, lust, sex are the main culprits responsible for a person's downfall because lust and sex create attachment. Attachment creates greed and when there is an obstacle in the way, anger is given birth. Lustful sexual desires are an enemy of all human-bodied beings, but only the wise tries to avoid it, or avoids indulging in it unnecessarily (other than for procreation).

An ordinary common man sees sex as the need and habit of the body, but the wise man sees it as the disease which binds us to this short-lived world and temporary relationships.

When a person is riding high on the tide of lust and *vasna*, he becomes a rapist. This is an animal instinct. In today's world, there are millions of perverts worldwide and burn with the fire of Lust, *vasna*, ruin lives of innocents. Hence they commit *adharma* which is a sin. *Adharma* leads him to destruction.

There is nothing wrong with lust until one seriously abuses himself because of lust. Anyone who is obsessed with lust is already living in hell.

There is a huge difference between lust and love, but this is hardly understood. Mistaking lust to be love can be said to be a serious tragedy of modern society. Lust sees the other person as an object for one's own enjoyment, while a true lover sees the other as 'life'.

If lust is combined with smiles, flattery and gifts, it cannot be considered as love. When we mistake ourselves to be physical bodies, whether male or female, we naturally come under the control of bodily drives for lustful pleasures. When relationships are formed based on lust, such relationships soon get destroyed. We start mistaking carnal love to be natural than spiritual love.

With no control over their senses, human beings fall under the sway of lust.

Lust is the manifestation of the mode of ignorance which leads to suffering. But when the same lust is transformed into devotional services, then lust becomes spiritualised. Spiritualised lust becomes our friend and not enemy.

Human form of life is a chance for the living entity to escape the entanglements of material existence. And the prime entanglement is lust. Human mind is full of lusty feelings and once it gets a chance, it erupts out. So, neglect the lusty feelings. Engage the mind in something worthy. Tolerate the urge for lust before it takes you to the path towards hell.

Suppression of desires is not the solution; transform desire to spirituality. This path is like Ayurvedic treatment which is slow but sure.

It is not easy, nor is it difficult. When our efforts are sincere, God protects us.

The devotee feels happier in being spiritual rather than being lusty.

Human beings can conquer the enemy, that is, lust by cultivating spirituality.

*'Do not shackle yourself in lust.'*

**Jealousy:** Jealousy is like most of the other emotions as it arises from within. Jealousy is all about not accepting good qualities in others, nor appreciating the person, the way, he/she is. Jealousy refers to thoughts or feeling of insecurity, fear and concern over a relative lack of possession. Jealousy can consist of one or more emotions, such as anger, resentment, inadequacy, helplessness or disgust.

Jealousy is a typical trait in human relationships. We see jealousy even in small babies. In infants, however, jealousy is natural and pure.

Jealousy is not something over which we have much control. It is a natural instinctive emotion that everyone experiences at some point or other. Its intensity is often deep-seated due to feelings of possessiveness and insecurity.

It is a complex emotion that includes a wide range of feelings, ranging from fear of abandonment to rage and humiliation. It strikes both men and women and is most typically aroused when a person perceives a threat, which may be real or imaginary. There are many root causes behind jealousy. One of the root causes is fear—the fear of being rejected and being left alone.

*'Lack of self- confidence: We are not confident in our abilities or skills.'*

*Insecurity:* A poor self-image and lack of self-confidence can result in making one feel insecure and this can be a strong reason for causing jealousy.

Situations arise where one experiences jealousy, as when someone achieves something that one may have always wanted to achieve or when someone one hates, succeeds. In many cases one feels jealous of the other, who manage to achieve something that one feels was not deserved by the other. A major part of the problem lies within us and not within the person who we are jealous of because the fear of losing someone or something to a rival creates anguish in us. When we battle insecurity in a relationship or in another person's achievements, it may come across as a threat to us. Jealousy itself can manifest as wicked presence in our lives.

Jealousy is a comparison—the other person has a better house, or a more beautiful body, or more money, or a more charismatic personality. The idea of comparison is pointless. If we keep on comparing ourselves with the others, then jealousy would be a natural outcome.

Envy and jealousy are closely related, yet there is a vast difference between them. Jealousy is not same as envy. Jealousy is resentment, while envy is at someone's success, achievements, advantages, etc. Envy denotes a longing to possess something awarded to, or achieved by another. Jealousy, on the other hand, denotes a feeling of resentment by *A* at *B* gaining something that *A* considers herself/himself to be more worthy of receiving. Everybody is jealous of everybody else and out of jealousy, we create hell. If the other is in misery, we feel good. If somebody loses, we feel good. If others are happy and successful, we feel bad. We become mean towards them.

By trying to put others down just because they are ahead of us is an indication of our weakness. We ought to try to place ourselves above others by our efforts to become successful. It is better to try and improve our life rather than getting jealous of others. If we experience jealousy in relationships, it means we are insecure about ourselves.

Excessive jealousy means there is a lot of fear. We must overcome our fears, be it the fear of rejection or fear of abandonment. By dealing with feelings of insecurity, we can reduce jealousy. Learning to deal with our fear is the basic step in dealing with jealousy. Control over anger is essential as it is directly related to jealousy. We have to learn to be assertive as it will help us in communicating without being aggressive or angry.

The main cause for jealousy is when we compare ourselves with others. Comparison is a very foolish attitude because each person is unique and incomparable. Once we understand this and stop comparing, jealousy will disappear.

Our life is small, so why make things tense? Try to be a more genuine person. Why do we want to be a carbon copy of others? We should learn to love ourselves and respect ourselves. The secret of happiness lies in accepting a situation the way it is, rather than the way you want it to be.

For this we need to build our self-confidence, know our strengths and soon would be worthy enough to eliminate all feelings of jealousy.

Also, our mental and physical self-image plays an important role. This will have a great impact on our self-confidence. It is due to jealousy that we are in constant suffering. We tend to become mean to others. If we continue to focus on jealousy, we will continue to suffer. We are not harming the person we are jealous of; rather, we are harming ourselves.

Jealousy will not allow us to move forward on our journey towards health. Jealousy is like a disease, a cancer of the soul as it remains in our subconscious mind.

Leave jealousy and never take it up again. Dropping

jealousy is blissful. Once we get rid of jealousy, we'll feel so very relaxed. By not being jealous of anybody, we will remain calm, happy and peaceful, thereby moving towards spirituality and tranquillity.

It is never too late to start. Start something different today. Why not be jealous of the people who are immersed in *bhakti?*

If anyone should be envied, it is them!!

Lord Krishna says:

*'Arjuna, because you are never envious of me, I shall impart to you this most confidential knowledge and realisation, on knowing which you shall be relieved of the miseries of material existence.'*

As Arjuna was not jealous, he became the receiver of *Gita ka gyana.* Envy and jealousy are rooted in ignorance; try to remove ignorance. We can purify traits like envy and jealousy by removing ignorance. As long as jealousy is not removed, the higher knowledge cannot be grasped. If we have the dark, negative seed in the form of jealousy inside us, we will not make progress in the spiritual world because God does not like people to suffer from jealousy. So, next time you feel the angst of jealousy creep inside you, think and identify the source of jealousy.

**Criticism:** Criticism is the practice of judging the merits and faults of something or someone. The expression of disapproval on the basis of perceived faults or mistakes is criticism.

While fault-finding may be an outcome of several mental states, it is often the mind's attempt to gain a superior position over others.

If we fall from our own identity, we feel superior to others by seeing faults in them and not in ourselves.

Criticism means negative gossip and it does not need any intelligence. We have to be egoistic. Criticism means satisfying our ego. It gives us a great feeling as it is very ego-fulfilling. By criticising others, we feel we are higher than others. It is the cheapest way to prove our superiority, to consider oneself somebody special, more knowledgeable, more intelligent.

By criticising others, we are being negative. Negativity must be made our approach as it leads to enlarging our ego. To make our ego bigger, the easiest way is to criticise everybody and complain against everything.

There is nothing pleasant about criticism if a critic is malicious because then he makes personal attacks. Most of the time criticism is done to motivate our own self by acquiring a sense of superiority or getting back at someone who has hurt you.

Sometimes we criticise others to avoid attention on our own shortcomings.

Negative criticism is very unpleasant and it sows a negative seed inside us. When we suffer, we say we have not done anything wrong in our life, but we forget that our negative behavior, our negative point of view about others, our habitual self-centred thinking and belief in our own self by criticising others is the main cause of our sufferings in life. We feel we are privileged to do so because we consider ourselves too big to give any importance to others.

Respecting the rights of others and allowing others to lead their lives as they wish is a good *karmic* action. We should desist from making mindless criticism of others.

Some people may be able to see only the negative side of others, so that they can highlight their own positive side.

Criticism is hurtful for most, but if justified, it can inspire both the critic and the critiqued.

Constructive criticism often involves exploration of the different side of an issue, or a person. Positive criticism draws attention to a good or positive aspect of someone that is being ignored or overlooked.

Positive point of view can be used as a technique to motivate, influence and help people to develop. Identifying our own motives takes honesty and courage. We need to have a strong desire to change.

We can ask ourselves, 'What is my motive for criticising others?'By changing our attitude and behaviour, we will gain an insight into the problem and then work diligently to correct it.

Be a self-critic and do your own self-assessment regularly. The closer you come to your own pure, original identity, the more you will show humility and freedom from seeing faults in others.

There are people who follow the rules strictly and avoid criticising others because they know criticism and fault-finding will create the bad *karmic* seed.

As we practice seeing good in others, we begin to feel calm and peaceful.

If we commit ourselves to practicing abstinence from fault-finding, we will reap the abundance of spiritual rewards that are sure to follow.

*'Be a self-critique.'*

**Judgemental:** Making a judgement means being judgmental. Judgmental means being over-critical. Judgmental is a negative word to describe someone who often rushes to judgement without any reason. The word describes someone who forms lots of opinions—usually harsh or critical ones—about others and in the process, we jump to our conclusions.

Being judgmental is a situation, an attitude, in which judgement about other people's conduct is made in an unhelpful way. We are quick to criticise people or tend to form opinions too quickly. We have a fixed negative attitude about something or someone.

It carries the meaning of *'passing judgement'*, black or

white, thumbs down or up. It focuses on the negative results in the process.

The cheapest way to feel good about oneself is by feeling superior to others. This bad *karmic* seed makes us judgmental. We divide others into categories of good and bad. When we are judging an another person, no matter how obviously they deserve the judgement, we must keep in mind that everyone is doing the best he can at his level of consciousness.

Sometimes it's a question of intent because we often make judgements based on biases. This may not justify their validity if they are based on false or distorted facts in either the individual or interpersonal relationship. An over--judgmental person will form opinions about people and situations very quickly, when it would be better for them to wait until they know more about the person or situation. Else they make judgements in a way that have harmful or negative consequences.

In a rush to condemn others, an overly judgmental person will not wait to gather all the facts, but will rush to his or her own conclusions. They then call themselves non-judgmental by claiming that it is only the abundance of faults in others, not their own desire to criticise.

Instead of accepting that nobody is perfect, a judgmental person feels wronged that someone else does not live up to expectation. And overly judgmental person will often have difficulty in accepting others' failures. These kinds of people have a negative, pessimistic attitude towards life.

Generally, people are too judgmental and have too much to say about other people. It is human nature, and yet, while it is in our nature to be judgmental, but it is not useful for us. We look down on others as if we are so much better and that creates division between people. We see someone based on their looks or actions; we pass judgement on them. We don't make an effort to get to know the person, or understand them or see whether a judgement was right or not. Instead of judging others, we should place ourselves in their shoes. We must try to accept that person the way he is without wanting him or her to change. When evaluating someone else's actions, let us remember to see where they are coming from and what is their perspective? For some people, the passing of judgement crosses the line of necessity of life for enjoyment.

An extra-judgmental person has difficulty in accepting things the way they are. Instead of viewing realty as it is, they prefer to simply reject those people and things they find threatening. Sometimes they do this just to exercise complete control over the situation. They forget that no single action can define someone and that a person's character is created through a lifetime of repeated actions, not a few isolated events.

Being extra-judgmental is a defence mechanism: By criticising others, we are protecting ourselves from a negative evaluation. We justify our judgment as 'the truth'. The judgement made by such people will often work in their favour. They tend to belittle the smart, intelligent people and sweep under the carpet their accomplishments as they have difficulty in accepting their strong personalities. Their intention are, if they let other people get close, they will end up hurting themselves. A judgemental person is generally threatened by others. So he tries to criticise others typically in order to elevate himself. He makes every effort to put others down as an over-judgmental person has a low self-esteem and lack of self-worth. By being judgmental, he builds negativity within. In this state of mind, he is not aware of the consequences of what he says or does. His ego makes him inattentive or absent for that moment. So one should not judge others mercilessly. Maybe it is because of jealousy towards that person.

Maybe this is the power in the form of money and status which make one feel privileged to judge others. One's ego, or *ahankar* is the root cause of one being judgmental. Such an arrogant person does not pay attention to the truth. Until we free ourselves from being judgemental, we can never understand the true aspect of the person whom we are judging. Possibly, we may have many other good qualities but being over-judgemental is negative and can be exhausting. So, if people around us start avoiding us, we must then ask ourselves if it is our criticism, ego and over-judgmental behavior which is responsible for being avoided. If we find ourselves in such a situation, we should check ourselves as we are not at ease with the society and the world. Constant criticism of others is certainly not appreciated. Those who engage in frequent judgements often feel an acute sense of selflessness, anxiety and depression.

So, if we find ourselves being judgmental, we should stop immediately and try to accept the person the way he or she is, without wanting him or her to change. Once we have accepted someone, we can try to love that person even if we have hated him or her in the past. Trust me, it can be life-changing. This calls for greater awareness. Hence avoid passing judgement and instead, build a bridge between yourself and others.

*'An over-judgmental person is not exactly fun to have around.'*

**Lie:** Causing someone to believe something that is not true and to do it intentionally is tantamount to lying. Lying is contrary to the nature of God as 'God is truth'. Telling a lie is the worst thing a person can do. Just to satisfy our hatred for someone, we tend to make false and damaging statements about others. We don't mind damaging someone's reputation by saying untrue things.

This may satisfy our ego but by doing so, we are sowing the worst kind of *karmic* seed inside us.

A lie does not become a truth just because it is told by you. In telling lies, we are not only harming others, we are harming ourselves much more because slowly we become incapable of knowing the truth itself. A person who tells lies can not believe that anyone can ever speak the truth. He is not able to trust anyone; he cannot make anyone his friend. He cannot take any matter in its natural form. Lying is a coward's way of getting out of trouble because sometimes it takes real courage and moral fibre to tell the truth.

For some it is a way of life. A habitual liar might tell a lie even when the truth would be easier, simply because he is used to doing it all the time. Lying causes such damage that it is sometimes impossible to correct it. It can hurt feelings and scar reputations. Not only can lying hurt other people, it can ruin the liar's own reputation.

'*Telling a lie is* adharma, *a very dark* karmic *seed.*'

**Gossip:** Whenever we say anything about someone in private and that which we cannot say publicly amounts to gossip. Casual conversations or reports about other people, typically involving details which are not confirmed as true, is gossip.

This would encourage people to start gossiping about you as soon as you leave. Gossip is idle talk or rumour, especially about the personal or private affairs of others.

Gossip is revealing the details about other people's lives behind their backs and also a few things extra, that aren't for sure real, merely to spice things up. Sometimes gossip is intentionally meant to harm someone in order to satisfy one's personal interest or purpose.

Gossip also means delving deep into the details of someone else's life and making it your business. A gossip-monger is a person who has privileged information about people and proceeds to reveal that information to those who have no business to know about it.

Generally, a gossip-monger speaks of the faults and failings of others, or reveals potentially embarrassing or shameful details regarding the lives of others, without their knowledge or approval.

What comes out of our mouth gives a picture of what is truly in our heart. If we are bitter, angry, or unforgiving, our words will probably not be full of love. Gossip-mongers do not always realise that they are gossiping. It is just a conversation for them. Gossip-mongers resort to this just to make themselves popular or feel important or derive advantage of some kind.

What is enjoyment for a gossip-mongers is criticism of someone and which can be done easily. We may just pick up the phone and start gossiping about others. We don't realise that by doing so, we are accumulating negativity in our life. Gossiping or speaking mindlessly about others when they are not present is the worst *karma* a person can do.

Individuals who are perceived to engage in gossiping regularly have less social power and are less liked. They are considered as less trustworthy after sharing a gossip. In fact, gossip is much worse than blackmailing somebody, as the gossip-monger exposes the personal and private secrets without a warning.

The exchange of gossip is negative most of the time. Of course, talking about other people's lives is not always negative, nor is it always gossip, but it can be a gateway for gossip. People without anything to do will eventually start talking about you. Gossip can turn a rumour into a fact and end in hurting people. Just remember that the things you say, be they in innocence, can end up by impacting somebody's life.

We should not slander another unintentionally or intentionally. So, we must be very mindful of the information we share about a person. Try not to speak about anyone when they are not there to defend themselves. If we do talk about other people, we should ensure that we don't taint another person's reputation in a way that it can never be remedied. Respect the fine line between giving vent to emotions and tarnishing the reputation as this is the greatest sin and a worst kind of *karma* anybody can do. Our bad intentions about someone else can one day come back to hurt us in the end!

People, whose lives lack meaning or purpose, often find interest in discussing the lives of others. Almost everybody gossips, but there are people who do not gossip. They are the ones who are awakened and have better things to do in life. They feel why should they waste time over gossiping when it is not their business. To behave like them, we have to be aware about what is right and what is wrong, or what is good and what is bad. When we do this, we start seeing the same people in a new light. Instead of gossiping, we feel immense compassion for the concerned person we used to gossip about earlier. Our outlook towards that person changes and we become more friendly.

Remember a gossip-monger jeopardises his chances of growth in life as he wastes his precious time and energy on idle gossip.

Try not to speak about anyone when they are not present to defend themselves. If we avoid participating in gossip, we will notice that the gossip disappears on its own.

*'Rise above gossip as it is a sin watched by God.'*

## Intention

*'Our intention is the most powerful tool at our disposal.'*

Intention is a state of mind which represents a commitment to carry out an action. Intention decides the fate of our action. While doing any *karma*, the **intention** behind it is important. It all depends on our intention every moment and determines what *karmic* seeds are being planted in our body and which seeds would ripen.

Intention means how we see ourselves and how we view others. To be more specific, *karma* refers to actions that are deliberate and willed, even if we do something instinctively without thinking about it, the unconscious intention is always behind it. So we should carefully pick and choose our intentions because while performing *karma*, intention plays a very significant role. *Karmic* consequences depend on our intentions.

*Now what is intention?*

Intention comes to the fore when we intentionally kill an insect and feel happy at killing it, while on the other hand, if we squash an insect by mistake and genuinely feel sorry at having killed the insect, then the intention is not there. So, here the *karmaphal* depends on our intentions.

On the other hand, there are some typical intentions that have nothing to do with goodness.

They are like wanting to be in control and have power over others or we want to be a winner in every situation. We want to make rules and want others to follow. All these intentions are egocentric and we mistake them for good intentions, forgetting that our ego has taken complete control over our mind. So, we carefully pick and choose our intentions because while performing *karma*, intention plays a significant role. Bad intention will harm us and not others.

In *kaliyuga*, the concept of God is misguided and there is no genuine teacher to explain what intention means in today's world. We ourselves have to understand the true meaning of intention.

False intentions are like a mask under which our intentions remain hidden. Our intentions always want others to fail in their efforts because we want to feel superior to others.

False intentions take the shape of meaningless desires. If we always live in the world of false intentions, we suffer from a feeling of fear, greed, rage which render us weak and helpless. We want to prove ourselves by taking risks even at the cost of our health and happiness.

We mistake our intention because our ego takes over complete control. If the intention is left to the ego, great tasks can be achieved but these are small achievements compared to what can be achieved with our unlimited intelligence, organising power and time management.

So set your intentions high and aim to be successful in life through good intentions; not egoistic intentions. If our intentions are ego-based, we get power, money, name and fame, but these intentions lead us to the path of materialism. These egocentric intentions trap us in their grip by making us feel 'in need' all the time. We always suffer from lack of materials. This sense of *lack* grows into hunger to achieve everything possible in sight.

Money, power, sex and worldly pleasures are expected to fill up this 'lack', but these never do so. This is what the ego-based intentions are. Our intentions should move in the direction of harmlessness and good thoughts inside us. If someone uses kind words but intends to snub, then that is the intention of the person from within.

The most expensive gift given without love has no meaning.

Our intentions in our life decide our fate. If we become manipulative and take advantage of the situation, we are definitely bound to generate a cycle of bad *karmas*.

So we must consult our inner self to understand what the reason is that prods us to act the way you do. This way we will be able to analyse the cause of our negative intentions. It depends on the level of inner depth that helps us to start deciphering the good and the bad intentions. This alone can prevent us from making dark seeds inside us. It is not difficult to avoid dark seeds as we are born with the potential to awaken ourselves.

By choosing the right intentions and by avoiding the dark seeds, we can attain the highest spiritual goal. If our intentions are spirituality based, we achieve inner growth, and this inner growth gives us peace and happiness.

It all depends on view of life. If we can nurture egoistic intentions, why can't we develop spiritual intentions?

The philosophy of *karma* is closely associated with intentions. Good intention creates good seeds while bad intention creates dark, negative seeds.

*'Karmaphal is wrapped within our intentions.'*

Intentions also refer to the spiritual principle of cause and effect, where intention and action of an individual influence the future of that individual.

If the basic intentions present within are honest, then God takes the responsibility for carrying them out in the form of peace and joy. Our intention is a foolproof plan for God, which He carries to completion in His own way. If our intentions are good, expect miracles from Him. To receive a reward from God, make sure to set your intention in the right direction and avoid egoistic intentions. Nobody can help us in this as we alone know when our intentions are honest and when they are superficial.

One good intention cannot carry us through life. It takes discipline to remind us day in and day out of our purpose in life. The only one reality which makes us peaceful and happy is our intention. In spiritual life, intention includes will and purpose, aspiration and a higher vision. If we set our intentions on God, we experience inner growth. If we set our intentions on materialism, the latter will grow into a dark seed. Once we plant the seed of our intention, our soul starts working on it accordingly.

*'Check your intentions before doing something.'*

*'Bad intentions will harm us, not others.'*

## Positive Seeds

*'Heaven on earth is possible if we choose our* karma *wisely.'*
For happiness in life, we should act according to Dharma without being attached to the fruits or consequences. Once we

decide to adopt this path, we will notice the change within us in the form of positive energy, which will direct us towards a wholesome state of mind. Right mindfulness is the key to attainment of serenity and insight. In this state of mind, we become aware about the consequences of what we say and what we do.

What happens around us is a mirror for what would happen around us, that is the sense in which we are responsible for all our life experiences, whether fantastic or unpleasant. Taking responsibility means to take ownership of the good and bad things we create, rather than constantly looking outside ourselves to find excuses.

Our *indriya* (senses) tells us what is right and what is wrong. We receive signals from our senses, but we refuse to pay attention to them. We refuse to believe that somebody inside us is preventing us to do bad deeds. We are so engrossed in the material world that we refuse to listen to the inner voice. There can be a perfect connection between the body, mind and soul but we are unable to understand this because we have so many layers of *kama, vaasna, moha, mamta* attachments which are masks and which prevent us from looking within. Our deeds and actions will not generate good *karmaphal* if we do them with an impure heart and falsehood. What is important is to remember that actions are not beneficial by themselves, but need to be accompanied with the virtue of good and pure thoughts.

For example, we must treat others the same way as we would want to be treated by others. The thing which hurts us will hurt others too. The proper role of *karma* is to look at others as you would look upon yourself. He who acts righteously is wise. We should not hurt or harm others by our thoughts and actions. We must avoid saying words that can pain others. As we apply the theory of positive *karma* to our own journey of transformation, we help to transform the consciousness of the people around us, our family, our social circle and even the world beyond.

## Conscious Efforts to Avoid Bad *Karmic* Seeds

'A karma *is a seed. We have to accept it deep down in our body (field) where it sprouts.'*

Ethically one's intentions, attitudes and desires count when evaluating one's actions. Through our positive deeds and actions, we can sow good *karmic* seeds. We should carefully and conscientiously fulfil our family, civil and spiritual duties by maintaining a perfect balance. When we lead a balanced life, we realise that liberation and freedom depend on our inner self rather than by becoming a *sannyasi* from outside. We are on the path of righteousness, if we know how to develop our character and what is our role in society.

Here are a few important factors.

**Ethical Earning :** Earning one's living in an ethical manner means right livelihood without manipulation and without harming anyone and anything. By following this principle we can sow a good *karmic* seed. We don't need to find an ethical career. We can make our earnings in an ethical manner. Any job we feel is going to harm our ethics should be avoided. That is called living in an ethical manner. We spend maximum number of hours in a day at the workplace. The potential for doing *karma* is therefore much greater. Our job must be legal and honest and should not harm others. Making profit at the cost of ethics should be a big no-no. We need to choose our profession carefully, honestly and harmlessly. If our job is unethical or we don't mind being unethical at work just because money is the only criterion, then this will sow the *karmic* seed of a worst kind. Running after money at any cost won't help us in leading a happy and peaceful life. What is the point of having so much unethically-earned money when we are unable to enjoy it due to ill health?

**Charity:** Doing charity is an attitude where we give material objects, time, energy and attention. Doing charity with our hard-earned money is very effective and is linked to good *karma*. On the other hand, when we have plenty of money but have no heart to donate to the needy, we are being mean-spirited and this creates bad *karma*. Learn to be detached from money through generosity. By donating we will develop a giving mind and this pleasure will keep us detached from the materialistic world. To give even a small amount from our hard-earned money causes seeds of goodness in this life and coming life to sprout. But giving should be done with good intention and with our hard-earned money for any benefit to accrue. Being generous, giving purely out of compassion, without expecting anything in return is true giving, which creates good *karmic* seeds. If we want to become wealthy, we have to be generous and learn the art of giving.

We should aim at providing benefit to others through our wealth. The selfish desire of reaping the benefits oneself will generate negative *karma* and render us poor.

**Patience:** Patience means all our successes require constant hard work. This means we need to be patient, regardless of the goals in our life. If we expect immediate results, we will ultimately be disappointed. Maybe our success is not big in comparison to what we are capable of achieving. But then, we have to figure out our true purpose and act in accordance with that purpose. In time, the expected success will follow.

**Respect:** Every person deserves consideration and respect. We cannot decide who is superior or inferior. Respect means to be empathetic towards others instead of dismissing them; respecting them makes them feel good. It makes them feel good about you and this generates good *karma*, making others comfortable. We always put ourselves ahead of everyone, not respecting and paying heed to the other person's needs.

**Let Go:** We carry a huge emotional baggage and most of it is filled with remorse, guilt, anger and jealousy. Going through life with so much negativity leads only to bad *karmic* seeds. No one but 'us', we alone can cure it. We need to learn to 'let go' and move on so that we can enjoy better things in life.

**Acceptance:** Acceptance is the key. Yes, we must accept our wrong doings and beg for forgiveness for all the wrongs we have committed in the past and learn from our actions.

**Good Gesture:** Do a good gesture because every little gesture counts and aids in generating good *karma*.

**Give Way:** Give way to others. We are impatient and think of ourselves as superior to everyone else. This causes unnecessary negativity, which leads to nothing and generates negative *karma*.

**Be Honest:** All people lie and often get their lies back in return. It may seem impossible to live a life without any deception at all. Telling white lies is an easy way of not hurting someone's feelings but being honest is a lot easier in any situation.

**Spread Positivity:** Giving spontaneous compliments is a great habit to cultivate or adopt. We must aim at spreading positivity wherever we go. If a person is in bad mood or sad, don't ignore them. Instead give a sincere compliment to them because complimenting someone proves very curative. Develop the habit of giving thanks and simply spreading positive vibes around you. Positivity is the key to a happier life.

**Kindness:** We cannot become kind because the person in front of us is someone we don't like. That does not mean we will insult that person. The situation is same for us as well. We must treat others the same way as we would want ourselves to be treated. If we want respect, we must give respect. Kindness should be our way of life in every aspect of life.

**Compromise:** We must never compromise on the principles of life.

Compromise means we are not certain; rather than compromising, we must abide by our principles. The more we compromise the less we become as an individual. We are a small part of the crowd; not an individual in our own personality, in our own right.

**Hospitality:** Providing a warm, friendly environment means hospitality. It means when someone makes us feel comfortable and at home even though he has not received a welcoming, friendly and warm treatment from us. This gesture, this behaviour of that someone amounts to hospitality. Hospitality is all about belief and practice. It suggests and encourages the importance and ensures that our actions reflect our deep belief in our practice. This practice is good and is a positive *karma* seed.

**Invest in Yourself:** Rather than getting into chaos of day-to-day routine which makes you lose sight of your own happiness, invest in yourself. When you take care of yourself, you are better prepared to take care of others and make meaningful contributions to the world.

We should not go through life without passion, be it anything. We can find a hobby, or ability, where we are able to succeed. It will elevate our self-esteem and we will feel better about ourself.

**Spend Time with Yourself:** Spending some time with one's self, i.e. alone or all by oneself in nature will help to introspect on one's actions and make 'a connect' with oneself. It helps us to acquire clarity and choose the path ahead. Spending some time with oneself helps in understanding the 'self' which keeps one away from generating bad *karmas*. We ought to learn to prioritise our life. Investing in oneself means feeling fulfilled and good about life and oneself.

**Stay Healthy:** We cannot control every aspect of our health. Sometimes illness will strike even people who have taken great pride in eating healthy and staying active. Still, take time out to ponder over your health as investing in health allows one to fully enjoy life.

**Read Scriptures:** Scriptures and holy books will help us understand the deeper meaning of life, help us make better decisions, enable us to see the good things in life around us. The new meaning of life will make us realise the futility of materialistic things.

**Chant a *Mantra:*** Chanting *mantras* helps to purify the negative imprints of *karma*, be it of the present life or the past life.

**Go on *Tirth Yatra:*** A visit to a holy destination has some significance. One feels a surge in one's energy that surrounds these places and helps the devotee on a spiritual level. The positive energy derived is infectious and helps us generate good, genuine thoughts.

**Meditate:** Meditation helps us to tune into our mind, focus on our inner being and clears our mind of unhealthy thoughts. It helps us understand our body and mind while connecting us with our soul. With a calmer mind, a person is able to make better choices.

**Live in the Present Moment:** If we cling too hard to the past feelings, experiences and beliefs, we will always have one foot in the past. Remember that the present is all we really have and that it is there to be fully engaged with and to be enjoyed. So, live in the present moment.

**Learn to say 'No':** Learn to say 'no' sometimes, so that you are not ruining yourself by trying to keep other people happy.

**Be Thankful to God:** Be thankful to God for everything you have in your life.

'God *loves attitude of gratitude*.' We should express gratitude to everyone who cares about us. Let them know how much they matter to us. Never take anything in life for granted, be honest and be thankful to God.

**Be Truthful:** Truth is nothing but God. Telling the truth is such a divine quality that it glorifies the human being. Humans must endeavour to uphold truth under all circumstances as God loves it. Truth is within us. Truth never hurts the teller; it is always the best policy to tell the truth because without it, we cannot maintain any relationship. The definition of truth may vary from person to person; however, it is generally something that a person believes in.

If the objective of telling the truth is to hurt someone then it is considered inferior to the worst lie. The truth that is spoken with bad intention is considered to be worse than a lie. Truth is purity that differentiates between right and wrong.

*'Truth is a statement that corresponds to reality and happiness which will set you free.'*

**Attitude of Gratitude:** An attitude of gratitude means making it a habit to express thankfulness and appreciation in all aspects of life on a regular basis, for both big and small things alike. Acknowledging other people's contributions and thanking them for their help and support leads to a better physical and mental health. Try adopting an attitude of gratitude to develop an overall and grateful mindset. This is the most impactful habit for leading a healthy life.

For some it is not easy to practice because of their ego; but we must drop our ego and practice the attitude of gratitude as it makes us feel as if it is the greatest blessing for mankind and which is within our reach. When a person is without gratitude, then something is missing in his life.

We must learn to thank God for everything in our life. When a man is content with his life, whatever it may be, without wishing for what he has not, his heart is filled with gratitude and he will receive heavenly blessings.

We need to thank God for the wonderful nature aound us, the beautiful life and we will start viewing everything with grateful eyes. This would bring a wonderful change in us. We will feel peaceful, content and happy. This is the path towards spirituality.

The attitude of gratitude is one of the most important habits for leading a fulfilling, healthy and happy life.

**Empathy:** To place oneself in another person's position is empathy. Empathy is the capacity to understand or feel what the other person might be is experiencing within. It gives us the ability to put ourselves in someone else's situation to see through his or her eyes. Acting requires the talent of empathy, the ability to feel another's emotions. An actor build his character by feeling the same emotions that a fictitious person would feel under certain circumstances. Empathy is a person's ability to share and understand each other's feelings. If we are capable of empathy, we can bond with those who are suffering, rejoice with those who are happy and feel pleasure at another person's achievements.

Empathy is a powerful tool which can make us kind as it gives us the ability to share and understand others' feelings. We give an opportunity to a loved one to talk about matters which are important to him. The most common reason why other people become angry is that they don't feel like they are being understood. Empathy is an attempt to understand the other person by getting to know his or her perspective. Empathetically reacting to another person can touch the person's heart, which builds trust and respect, allows the release of emotions, reduces tension and makes one happier.

Empathy has many benefits. The pleasure centres of the brain light up when we are empathetically heard and understood. It fosters resilience, trust, healing and nourishing connection. It is a quality which, when mastered and correctly used, can help transform negativity into a positive attitude and behaviour by building trust. It leads to forgiveness and imparts greater satisfaction in any relationship. It is a path towards consciousness. It increases one's altruistic behaviour and those lacking empathy cannot progress spiritually. Empathy gives a sense of purpose and the reason to be alive in the world. Without empathy, our creative thinking is limited by our own experience and perspective.

**Compassion and Sympathy:** Compassion is the ability to understand the emotional state of another person or of oneself. Compassion literally means *'to suffer together'*. Compassion motivates people to go out of their way to help the physical, mental or emotional pains of another. Compassion involves more than putting oneself in another's position. Often confused with empathy, the word compassion has the added element of having the desire to alleviate or reduce the suffering of another, while empathy is the ability to put oneself in the other person's place. Compassion arises through empathy and is characterised by action. We don't need to wait for a crisis to put compassion into action.

The sympathetic person is one who is motivated by compassion. Sympathy is feeling compassion, sorrow, or pity for the hardships that another person is undergoing. There is a difference between sympathy and empathy. Sympathy is when we share the feelings of another; empathy is when we understand the feelings of another but do not necessarily share them.

The people who work for Red Cross and similar voluntary organisations are sympathetic people.

**Ways to show compassion**

- Practice acts of kindness
- Incorporate a 'thank you' in your daily routine
- Say encouraging words
- Motivate others
- Praise others
- Share a hug
- Smile more
- Respect privacy
- Encourage others

## Loving Nature is a Positive *Karma*

Nature or *prakriti* is the only real force that exists and therefore, it is the most powerful force in existence. The word 'nature' is used for all the things that are normally not manmade. Nature is the natural, physical, or material world or universe. Nature rules our planet. The power of *prakriti* is the fragrance of the **earth**, the coolness of running **water**, the warmth of the raging **fire**, the softness of the blowing **air** as a breeze and the depth of the **sky** or the space towards infinity.

Nature includes animals, forests, rivers, oceans, mountains, soil, waterfalls and other things in the world that are not made by humans. The most amazing thing about nature is its infinite variety, like trees, grass, the ecological balance, the natural unspoiled scenery of the countryside, all of which are natural phenomena as distinct from human beings and their creations.

Humans can do many great things but compared to nature, we are nowhere. The universal nature is more powerful than any manmade force in existence. The question should not be how powerful nature is for it can never be underestimated. Tornadoes, super volcanoes, earthquakes, floods, etc. have enough explosive power to destroy the earth. Nature can move mountains, create havoc by destroying population, erode rocks and cause all kinds of destruction, while, at the same time, it can grow amazing greenery, provide unspoilt landscape or countryside, beautiful falls, amazing beaches, breathtaking hills and so on.

Nature is very powerful and should not be underestimated as it makes her presence felt in many ways. Mother Nature is sometimes used to refer to nature, especially when it is considered as a force that affects human beings. *Maya*, *Shakti*, *Prakriti* are its various names and we must respect and love nature.

## Be environment-friendly

Environment-friendly means not being harmful to the environment. Eco-friendly literally means 'earth friendly' and commonly refers to green living or practices that help conserve resources like water and energy. We can engage in eco-friendly habits or practices by being more conscious of how we use our resources. Many people want to lead a more sustainable life and to conserve the planet's resources by operating in a way that does not harm the environment. 'Going green' and saving energy and water are a few terms which refer to the guidelines and policies that refer to reduced, minimal and no harm upon ecosystems or the environment. Ecofriendly has become a buzzword. By understanding the true meaning of 'green living' and being ecofriendly, we can implement the practices that will lead to healthier living for the planet and its habitants, big or small.

## Collective *Karma*

We live in a society where we live in a small community but within a large society; so we all share a collective *karma*. This *karma* is created through intention, just as individual *karma* is. As we already know, individual *karmas* are motivated by selfish desire aimed at personal gain and at the expense of others. Similarly in a society, those in power, operate for material gain for themselves rather than from the sense of civic duty. They may find ways to break the laws for their own benefit.

The worst kind of *karma* against nature and environment is by allowing industries to throw toxic waste in rivers, which poses a danger to the environment and public health. Industrialists are not bothered about toxic wastes for by releasing effluents in rivers, they can maximise their profits. They know how to find ways to get away with it by using their money power.

Unauthorised construction poses a big hazard to the environment. Burning fossil fuels causes air pollution through release of toxic gases, which not only contribute to climate change but also raise the earth's temperature.

Nature and environment are the most important resources of life. A clean environment is essential for healthy living; therefore, we should keep our environment clean and protected. People and society should practice green environmentalism to save mankind as well as our coming generations.

*'Be a nature lover.'*

## *Karma* in Relationship

*'One can remain unattached and innocent in the midst of relationships by following* karmayoga, *selfless* karma.'

Relationships lie at the heart of most of our significant life experiences. They help to nurture our body and soul and teach us important lessons. They help us to see and understand ourselves through the eyes of others. Our main source of learning is through relationships. We learn joy and sorrow when we share these with others. How we are doing, what lessons have been learnt, are a field test to determine our progress in life. Do we reach out to others with understanding, love and compassion, or do we reach with fear, selfishness or rejection? Without relationships, we would not know ourselves nor can we test our progress.

We live in a society where everyone needs friendship and love. We share our life with many other relationships—our parents, siblings, children, friends and lovers, in different ways. A true friendship in life can make it easier to cherish all other relationships in life. If we are lucky enough to get a friend, we should consider ourselves rich.

Suddenly we experience a deep bond of friendship which was unknown to us and about which we had no idea—a friendship between two of us suddenly developing with another. Many a time it happens that our best friend whom we had loved a lot, now means nothing to us. These cases show that friends can become enemies, lovers can become strangers and people to whom we are indifferent can become friends. Maybe this is a *karmic* connection.

All relationships continue or die, so let them die easily when their time is up. Trying to hold on to anything or anyone is meaningless. Although the relationship is over, the friendship and love we may have experienced remains in our heart. Think of the relationship fondly and thank the friend for sharing time with you. Accept the situation and move on with grace, love and dignity. Wish them well and let them go. Don't gossip about them. This will avoid bad *karma*. Act pleasantly towards them which will help you in becoming detached towards friend and the relationship, enabling you to lead a stress-free life.

Love can be destructive as well as fulfilling. In love, generally people are attracted to the outer appearance without realising that beauty fades away while true love remains. Often, what happens that our best friend whom we loved so much, now means nothing to us, because we mixed up love with lust. There is a very fine line between lust and love. Love is not lust. Don't confuse sexual desire with love. A true friend is very difficult to get. Consider yourself very lucky if you get a true friend.

Living life with a warm heart and kind feelings towards everyone creates the *karma* which leads to love and happiness. Though we want to be nice to everyone, but it is difficult to please everyone. When people are nice to us, it is easy to feel love for them, but when someone is unkind, it is difficult to feel love and affection in return. Developing a loving attitude towards those we feel indifferent to, or we dislike, is difficult.

We sometimes find our moments of happiness ruined by someone's criticism. Even though we know that the other person's actions and words are due to jealousy or a feeling of inferiority, or any number of reasons, we still have that unhappy feeling. It is a very few people who love to take away someone's happiness.

To avoid bad *karma* in a relationship, it is advisable to treat and cherish everyone as our own but when we encounter someone who is making life difficult or unpleasant for us, try to cope with it, but if we are unable to do that, then we must withdraw ourself from the relationship. We must not talk ill about others behind their back in order to avoid bad *karma*.

We may not like or feel a connection with everyone we meet, or we know, but a dignified approach towards them will help us to lead a guilt-free life. By withdrawing ourselves from such a relationship we will be able to lead a very peaceful life.

Attachment and ego are very powerful impulses in a major relationship, such as between parents and children. It has different phases, such as unconditional love and fulfilling our responsibilities towards children when they are children. Now the time comes when the child grows up and becomes his own self. They ought to be given their freedom, instead of controlling them. At this stage, children should not take the parent-child relationship for granted. Children should not forget that parents have contributed towards their happiness and well-being through their selfless efforts and behaviour. Maybe parents don't need their children to help them financially but emotionally, yes. They need children's love and respect.

A time comes when a situation arises when something happens which we had never imagined. We have to accept the situation as a *karmic* effect or the previous birth's *karma*. To break this *karmic* chain, we must do *nishkam karma,* accept the unavoidable situation and do our duty as parents.

Trust me, God is there to give us wisdom to handle the situation wisely and this can be helpful in our spiritual growth. Accept this as a *karmic* result of our relationship in previous life.

If we really love our children, then let them go. Give them adequate space to be themselves. If we give our children space to be what they desire to be, then both the parents and children and their relationship can flourish. If we want to break this *karmic* chain of a bad relationship between us and the child, then get detached. Attachment demands return from children. If we want to be happy, we need not cling to our children. Don't be insecure. Detachment gives space to the other person and is trusting while attachment or too much dependency can be claustrophobic and painful. So, let go off your attachment to avoid feeling disappointed later.

Don't expect happiness from your children; rather accept your own responsibility to stay happy. Don't hold someone else responsible for your suffering or your happiness. Being attached is not an expression of love. Staying detached and still loving the children is a truly spiritual behaviour, which is akin to doing *karma* without expecting love in return. The essence of healthy relationship with the children is respect and that we can spend quality time with each other, enjoying each other's company.

We should never impose ourselves on them by reminding them about our unselfish contribution to their happiness and well-being. We cannot expect our children to fulfill our needs financially or emotionally. Make yourself self-reliant, so that you are not a burden on them in your old age. This aspect makes the parent-child relationship very comfortable that there is no financial liability on the child. Relationships need nurturing and attention. A soulful relationship comes from the heart and not the head. When in doubt, choose the heart. People can be good friends but need not necessarily be soul-mates. Allow the soul to enter the relationship through awareness and understanding.

*'A soulful relationship brings true joy in our life.'*

□

# Bhaktiyoga

*'God has so much surplus that He wants to distribute it.'*

## Bhaktiyoga

I personally chose *bhakti* to lessen my sufferings when I lost my daughter Neha.

I went into depression and my mother advised me to pray. I wanted to break my *karmic* chain through the *bhakti marg.*

Prayers have been used extensively over the centuries to help train the mind to think positively. Self-less *bhakti* helps us to purify negative thinking and lead the mind towards a positive approach in life. Sincere and regular *bhakti* creates good *karma*, leading to *gyana*, which helps us to perform *nishkam* (selfless) *karma. Bhakti* alleviates our suffering by making us detached and free from anger.

*Bhakti* means 'to be fulfilled in oneself' and that makes us feel complete. There is no need for us to go anywhere. When a person stays wholly within himself in *bhakti*, it can be a very fortunate happening. Prayers mean a deep sense of involvement while *bhakti* means a constant flow of thoughts of the divine within every moment of the day. *Bhakti* is not something which we can do at our own convenience; it is a continuous remembrance. When it starts, it never ends, but continues endlessly. In the material world, the people are so busy doing other things that they have no time for *bhakti*. *Bhakti* is last on their list of priorities; the last necessity which never gets fulfilled.

The meaning of *bhakti* should be understood. Many people pray but do so superficially. They go and attend a *satsang,* which is in reality nothing else but a meeting place or an occasion for enjoyment.

*Bhakti* entails singing God's name through deep feelings as the path of *bhakti* is done through the heart and not through the head. The *satsang* should create detachment in us. The *satsang* which creates attachment to people or things cannot be a *satsang*. *Satsang* means search for the truth.

If we want to break the *karmic* chain, we need to do *sattvic bhakti* or prayer to God without expecting anything in return. It is a great challenge. We have to work hard for it. We must do *sadhana*, pray and make an effort towards knowing God. This journey is very laborious and only those who are ready to cross all difficulties, can take to the divine path. It is not easy to get this. We have to work for it. God's *kripa* (benevolence) is showered only on those who have worked for it without any expectation. When we surrender ourselves completely to the divine, then God takes care of his *bhakt* (devotee).

*Bhakti* involves that no matter what we do, we should always think of God. If we pray to God everywhere and under all types of circumstances, it is known as *bhakti*. *Bhakti* is not what is visible; what is visible is not everything. There is also that which cannot be seen, that which is invisible. *Bhakti* is to remember the invisible always.

All relationships in this world are selfish and shallow. There is no depth in these relationships, but a relationship with the divine will bring love in reciprocation from Him. People on this earth deceive most of the time. It is better to be in the company of God, who can be with us always. Do not spend your time on doing what is futile. If we visit the temple, it is for all the wrong reasons. Someone goes there asking for a job, some for money, some for a life partner and some for a son. There is no point in going to the temple for all the wrong reasons. We can never come out of our desires as we do not realise that we are taking the entire burden of our worries, desires with us to the temple.

The temple is not a place; it is a state of mind. There can be no temple as long as it is accompanied with a demand. We are in the habit of visiting the temple to ask for some petty thing. Only that person, who goes to the temple, *not to ask, but to thank,* knows the real meaning of *bhakti*. One who has understood that by asking, one does not get anything except misery, **can reach the temple**. One who understands that a beggar's bowl is always empty, in spite of continuously asking it, is never full. A person who has understood that asking for anything is in vain will never ask for anything.

Only that person, who visits the temple to thank God for every little gift he receives, knows the real meaning of *bhakti*, the real meaning of temple. True *bhakti* fills us with gratitude. In this state of gratitude, the feeling of gratitude within is actually true *bhakti*. It means we know the meaning of going to the temple. True and *sattvic bhakti* gives us more than what we deserve. God's grace is abundant and the divine power showers His Grace upon us. We notice that we have not earned as much as what we have received. God has so much surplus that He is ready to distribute. After receiving so much, how can we be a miser in thanking Him. When we visit the temple, instead of thanking Him, we tend to complain that God is not hearing our demands; He is not fulfilling our desires. If we pray but want returns, then this kind of prayer becomes an obstacle on the path to reach God.

Expecting God to fulfill our desires because we have done so much while praying or having lit so many *diyas* and *agarbattis* (lighting lamps and incense) or offering so many flowers, we cannot expect anything in return as it shows that our prayers were done with a selfish motive. Praying and expecting something in return cannot be considered *sattvic bhakti.*

We visit the temple to pray to God, but our thoughts are not with God. We are thinking about our business and how to make more money or thinking about our enemies and how to harm them. There is no need to go to the temple. By not visiting the temple we will not earn bad *karma*, but while praying without concentration means accumulation of negative *karma*. While praying in the morning, we promise ourselves that we will not do any negative *karma* today, but as soon as we start our work, we repeat the same thing. We only think about business, not about God when we are in the temple.

*Sattvic bhakti* means, not quantitative *bhakti*, but qualitative *bhakti*. *Bhakti* is not mathematics; even one minute of our prayer from the heart is enough, if done with deep respect and love for God. God can hear us if our heart is in the prayer. He trusts the truth in our prayers. He has no doubts in our prayers. God will listen to our prayers. We have to be sincere in our effort.

*Bhakti* is our faith in God. If our *bhakti* is *nishkam*, we begin to have faith in ourselves and it makes our life free from turmoil and distress. *Bhakti* gives us inner knowledge and we get to learn of God's ways. Faith in God tells us that He will support us in every situation and this faith in God can even move mountains.

*Bhakti* is a journey that takes us to a place that is different from material thoughts. As we become serious about our *bhakti* and do it with *Sattvic shraddha*, every prayer gets answered. Prayer has the power to alter the outward events on a miraculous level. But it all depends on our consciousness. If we pray without *shraddha,* then our selfish prayers will not be able to create any result.

*Bhakti* does not condemn any aspect of a materialistic life. As far as material necessities are concerned, human beings at the present moment are very much ahead in living comfortably, but still we are not happy because we are missing the point. The material comforts of life alone are not sufficient to make us happy; the root cause of our dissatisfaction is that our dormant loving attitude has not been fulfilled despite our great advancement in the materialistic way of life. *Bhakti* teaches us how to live in this material world, perfectly engage in devotional service and thus fulfil all our desires in this life and the next.

*Bhakti* does not mean condemning the material world but means to teach and learn the art of loving God. *Bhakti* teaches us the science of loving every one of the living entities perfectly by the easy method of loving God. The method is very simple, but one has to understand it with a cool head. The method is to pour water on the root of a tree or supply food to the stomach. This is a universally scientific and practical method. Everyone knows that when we eat food or when we take in food into the stomach, the energy created by that food is immediately distributed throughout the whole body. Similarly, when we pour water on the root of a tree, the energy thus created is immediately distributed throughout the complete tree or even the largest tree. It is not possible to water every part of the tree or feed the different parts of the body separately.

In today's world, we are trying to keep ourselves happy by all means, *but we are neglecting to water the root, i.e. God.* If we miss this point it means missing oneself also. If we learn how to love God, then it is very easy to immediately love every other relationship and cvcry living being. *Bhakti* teaches us that there is only one root that will immediately spread happiness, and that is God. One who does not understand this simple science is missing the point in life.

*Bhakti* is sometimes understood to entail ritualistic activities. There are people who restrict themselves to rituals described in the *Vedas* as *karmakand.* But if one becomes attracted simply to rituals, without understanding the true meaning of *bhakti*, is indulging in selfish activities.

He performs the Vedic rituals, the *karmakand*, only to gain material achievements. If *bhakti* is not devoid of all material desires, then it is like praying with the materially-contaminated sense/*indriya*. So the result of such *bhakti* is also contaminated. When the same *indriya* are engaged with a pure heart, without any desire or attachment, then it is called pure *bhakti* or *nishkam bhakti*.

In *bhakti* it does not matter which family or society or nation one belongs to. We may be a Brahmin or a Shudra or maybe possessing a high-status, we must realise that loving God is akin to loving everyone. This way we can put ourselves on the path of transcendental pleasure. When our *bhakti* is pure, it brings immediate relief from all kinds of material distress.

*Nishkam bhakti* marks the beginning of attracting goodness and joy in our life, but *nishkam bhakti* is very rarely achieved in *kaliyuga*. It requires complete surrender to the divine. We cannot attain peace and bliss without putting in sustained efforts. God is found through untiring efforts, disciplined life, *sattvic bhakti* and *nishkam karmayoga*. We have to surrender ourselves wholeheartedly and then His divine grace is showered upon us. A *nishkam bhakt* does not ask for anything material; all he wants is God's *kripa* (benevolence), His Grace and His blessings.

God is always attained through grace. When a *bhakt* surrenders himself to the divine completely, then he does not do anything by himself. He does whatever the divine makes him to do. He entrusts himself fully in the hands of God. No longer does he have any name of his own. For him *bhakti* means complete and ultimate surrender.

*Bhakti* is a seed which is beautiful because happiness blooms out of it. When the *bhakti* seed sprouts, it makes us feel peaceful, contented and joyful. So, we must clean the ground of our inner self before sowing the seeds of love, devotion and pure *bhakti*.

It takes time to clear the layers of material pleasure. But to reach this state, we have to put in a lot of effort. If we want to try this path, we should not forsake our efforts midway.

Sometimes we start with *bhakti* and meditation with full enthusiasm. We do it for a few weeks and then forget about it. If we get into the habit of giving up, then all the efforts are wasted. Continuity and discipline are needed on the *bhakti marg*.

*Nishkam bhakti* is the only means, the only way, to attract God. This means that *bhakti* is stronger than God Himself, but pure and *nishkam bhakti* is very rarely achieved. It is not possible until one surrenders unto Him, giving up all other desires. Those in pure devotional service often forgo even the concept of liberation. Krishna gives his word to the *nishkam bhakt* that he will protect the surrendered soul from the reactions of sinful activities. But for that, complete surrender is necessary.

Pure *bhakti* implies freedom from the desire of any material benefit and to pray to God without expecting any return. This *bhakti* is known when one surrenders completely without any doubts in mind and without any expectation in return. Even expecting transcendental realisation or spiritual attainment through *bhakti* is akin to '*asking*' for something in return from God. *Bhakti* must always be free from any expectation of a positive result. Our prayers must always be free from such selfish desires. Our *bhakti* should always include spontaneous and loving service without any plans to reach God.

Most people meditate and pray because they have learnt that by practising *kriya,* they will attain spirituality. This is nothing short of expectation. We are meditating and doing *kriya* so that we can become spiritual as told by our *gurus* to us. We are spending hours and hours doing this, but the result is a naught, absolutely nothing.

It is because we are always thinking of the result to achieve from the *kriya* practice and meditation. This is a planned procedure, which is not spontaneous and loving service to God. It is also not *nishkam bhakti* as there is a desire attached to it. And when there is desire attached, it cannot be called selfless devotion or service to God. We are not pleasing God; rather we are pleasing ourselves at the thought that we are spending so much time to please God. We are attached to our efforts.

By following our *guru* or spiritual master, the connection between us and our *guru* is more and the actual connection with God is less. We are thinking and talking about our *guru* all the time. We are praying our *guru* more than God by offering our services to the *guru's* picture. The *guru* is present in our mind all the time. So, where is the place for God in our busy mind? We are spending hours in *satsang*, hours in meditation and longing for our *guru's* company all the time. So where is God in it?

If we spend a little time by pondering on God with a pure heart and mind, we will see God. A *sakshatkar* will happen in life and we will experience God on a regular basis without going to a temple, a *satsang* or any *guru*.

As Krishna says:

*'Those, who follow this path of devotional service and who completely engage themselves in faith, making Me the supreme goal, are very dear to me.'*

On accepting the *bhakti marg*, we need not bother about material goods to look after ourself and our family, because by the grace of God, everything is taken care of automatically. Anybody who does *nishkam bhakti* can attain *amrit (*nectar) by engaging in the service of God. To get this nectar, we need not belong to the family of a Brahmin. Any caste can elevate itself by engaging in *bhakti* to attain the *amrit-rasa.*

An ordinary family man, who works hard day and night and is successful in providing comforts for the members of his family, is very happy and enjoys every bit of it, but his entire collection of material happiness exhausts itself along with his body, as soon as life gets over. At death, everything ends and one must begin a new chapter of life in a new situation, perhaps a higher or a lower one than the last one. However powerful you are in any field of activity—political, social, national or international—the result of our actions will get over with the end of life. This is certain and nobody can alter this fact.

While on the other side, the *bhakti-rasa*, the *amrit* you have drunk by doing *nishkam bhakti*, does not end with the end of life. It continues and goes with you after your death. This *amrit* does not die but exists eternally. Material activities and their results end with the body; *bhakti* gives a chance in the next life of being born again as a human being.

As Krishna says:

'*A little advancement in bhakti can save the devotee from the greatest danger*'- missing the opportunity to be a human being in the next birth.

Any form of material or social acquisition cannot guarantee that one's next birth will be as a human being. While a person engaged in *bhaktiyoga*, even if unable to complete the course of *bhaktiyoga*, will take birth in the highest form so that he can automatically further his advancement in *bhaktiyoga* as mentioned by Krishna in the *Bhagavad Gita*.

So, all efforts in *bhakti marg* are *amrit* or nectar. This path will immediately bring one to the sacred life, free from sufferings and will bless one with 'beyond physical human experience into a spiritual area'. With this path alone, we can experience *out of body experiences*, which are more than liberation. *Bhaktiyoga* itself is sufficient to produce a feeling of liberation because it attracts the attention of the supreme Lord directly.

We cannot know God as God cannot be seen if our *indriya* (senses) are materially blunt. The process of pure *bhakti* will gradually transfer us from the material attachments in life to a spiritual status. Being constantly involved in *bhakti* can purify our *indriya* and when we pray with our pure senses, then the *bhakt* gets immersed in *bhakti-rasa*, enjoying every moment of life and relishing every bit of it. For this process, we need wisdom. If a person is wise, a true *gyani*, he can achieve liberation from the material world because he has understood that attachment is the root cause of all sufferings. But still, all such efforts can hardly offer anyone pleasure to do *sakshatkar*. We may try such processes for many, many thousands of births, but still we would be unable to attain the pleasure of *sakshatkar*. One must be blessed by God to undergo that experience. With God's *kripa*, one can experience *sakshatkar*; there is no other way.

Pure *bhakti* is dependent on God's *kripa* and for that, we must surrender ourselves completely. No one can enter that stage unless the door is opened by a *bhakt*. Lord Krishna gives *Gita ka gyan,* but Arjuna is still not sure and keeps questioning one after another. If our acceptance of God is without any doubt, then it becomes *nishkam bhakti*. No one can help us in this as God can offer us anything but *nishkaam bhakti* as it comes under the will power of a *bhakt*. He does not think about material gains. For him, any desire except service of Lord is called material desire. God is everything, the cause of all causes; therefore the *bhakt* surrenders himself completely to Him.

Krishna tells Arjuna: *'You can declare to the world, I will protect my pure devotee.'*

## Logic in *Bhakti*

God cannot be attained through logic, analysis or thinking. Pure *bhakti* is impossible if we find logic in everything. *Bhakti* is the language of the heart, so we should not search for logic or intellect in it. *Bhakti* can be done only through the heart and not through your mind or logic. If we try to see logic in everything, we cannot hear the language of God. A mind which is endowed with intelligence cannot understand the essence of *bhakti*. People, who depend too much on logic, will find one day that logic can become the cause of their downfall. Logic means false intellect. It can be used both ways. One is a believer in God and the other is an atheist. Both of them depend on their logic, but the victory of logic is no victory at all. One who is defeated with love is really defeated.

*Bhakti* has not to be performed with thinking, but with feelings. *Bhakti* has not to be done with logic, scriptures or principles, but with an open heart. Do not overburden yourself with logic. If our head is very heavy with logic, we won't be able to understand the language of love and even if we were to try, our logic will not allow us to see any sense in it.

A logician cannot do *bhakti* because prayers can be recited only by a lover of God from the depths of his heart. Try to remove layers of logic, so that the light of truth becomes visible. Victory of logic is no victory. If we were to think that, then we would be fooling ourselves. It takes time to clear the layers of false intellect. The new house can be built only after demolishing the old one. Once the old house of logic is destroyed, we can build the new house with love and feelings. When the flower of *bhakti* blossoms, then the sun of truth shines on it. This is the true meaning of *bhakti*. If we can understand this properly, then we will see God everywhere in our life, but if we want to know this through logic, we will never attain God.

Don't go on logics; don't doubt divine power.

Logic is very small; it is the method of a small mind. That is why they miss out on so many things in their lives. Their minds keep on adding things up and make life logical, but life is not plus and minus. Life is not a calculation. There is no substitute to living a logic-free life. We need to leave logic aside to attain spiritual awareness. Logic does not have any strength of its own. It can be used on both sides—for and against anything. Logic does not belong to anyone, so do not depend too much on logic. In *bhakti-marg*, it can become the cause of one's downfall. Do not doubt too much.

Krishna says:

*'Surrender yourself completely to the divine without any doubts and logics.'*

Doubtful persons have no status and they fall. Those who have no faith and are always doubtful about God and scriptures, make no progress at all. For the doubting soul, there is happiness neither in this world nor in the world behind.

## God is Gracious

God has so much surplus that he wants to distribute it to us all in the form of happiness. There is so much bliss that it is overflowing, so it needs to be given. God has given us doors with such unique possibilities that we can see beauty with our eyes, can hear beautiful music with ears, hands to feel the touch of life, a mind to understand, a heart to feel love and joy, a life to live and enjoy nature, the world. After receiving so much in abundance, we behave miserly in thanking Him. When we enter the temple, instead of thanking Him, we complain that God is not hearing our demands and not fulfilling our desires.

Generally, people say, "I pray and worship, have lit so many *diyas* and *agarbattis* (lamps and incense), offered so many flowers, fasted and meditated, but have failed to obtain any results to my prayers. The desire to seek some benefit in return is the obstacle in attaining happiness. We may do everything while praying, perform all kinds of rituals, but while doing so, we had been expecting something in return.

God hears us if our heart is in our prayers. We cannot harbour doubts in our prayers; God will listen to our prayers if we are honest.

God is not found in a temple but within oneself. It is not hidden in the mountains. If we go in search of Him, we will not find Him. We will not be able to attain God while we go on running after it. God is not somewhere outside. We have to look for God within ourselves. We don't have to go anywhere; God appears wherever we are. If we understand this, then everything happens that very moment! God Himself showers His divine blessings on us. *God also needs a true bhakt. He is also searching for a genuine bhakt. God is nothing without a bhakt.*

God is needed when we are helpless and in that state of helplessness, when we call Him through prayers and *shlokas* or *mantras*, then that becomes devotion. An accessible place beyond material reality is a prayer, a journey that takes us to a place different from ordinary thoughts. Prayer is our faith in God. If our prayers are selfless, we begin to have faith in ourselves. This faith can make an impossible possible.

## Power of *mantras*

*'Our* mantras *are very powerful.'*

When we chant the holy *mantras*, we directly communicate with God. One must chant the holy *mantras* as often as possible, anywhere and anytime of the day. We can set a specific time of the day to regularly chant the *mantras*. Early morning hours are ideal. I personally do *jaap*, recite the *mantra* softly. Concentrate on hearing the sound of the holy mantras. As we chant, we can pronounce the *mantras* clearly. If our mind wanders, bring it back to the sound of the *mantra*. The more attentively and sincerely we chant the *mantras*, the more spiritual progress we will make.

Our *mantras* are very powerful because God has invested all His powers in them. We can do *jaap* (chant *mantras*) on *jaap* beads (string). This only helps to fix our attention on the *mantras. Jaap* can be done alone in the house, in a peaceful atmosphere. There are no hard and fast rules for chanting *mantras*, but if we commit ourself to daily *jaap* in the morning and evening, it will earn us the best result. Negativity starts getting diminished gradually by chanting *mantras*.

*Jaap* of *mantras* is like watering the root of a tree. It is not possible to water every part of the tree. Similarly, when we do *jaap*, the energy created by it is immediately distributed throughout the whole body. *Jaap* is one switch that will immediately brighten up everything. By doing *jaap* regularly, a devotee realises the presence of God.

As we become serious about praying and do it regularly with *shraddha*, every prayer is answered. *Mantra* has the power to alter outward events at the level of miracles. Finally, when we have reached the state of soul consciousness, our every thought becomes a prayer, even if we are not doing *jaap*.

## *Bhakti*—Loving God

Until our infatuation with the material world gets over, we cannot do *bhakti*. This infatuation is the cause of our misery. This is not going to help us in any manner.

A devotee realises the presence of God by doing intense *nishkam bhakti*, while a materialist cannot remain either in the sense pleasure or in renunciation. He cannot be happy in either state. Sense enjoyment does not stay for long; it diminishes with time and age and as death nears which is in any case inescapable. So, our love with materialism gets over with our body.

Think about the art of eternal love. We can call it a special kind of love—the spiritual love between an individual soul and the Supreme Soul. Connection between *atma* and *paramatma* is the only love that is truly eternal. It does not end with the end of life.

The basic principle of life is that we have a tendency to love someone. No one can live without loving someone else. In the primary stage, a child loves his parents, then his brothers and sisters, his family, society, his country, even the whole human society. But the love is not satiated even by loving everyone. The reason is that we need to invest so much time and energy to love everyone. If we could learn the art of loving God, then we can learn to love everyone and everything. This process will bring us the maximum happiness because it is not possible to water the tree, part by part. When we start loving God, we start loving all. We love our relations, friends, society, nation. We love nature and become environment-friendly; we realise the meaning of do's and don'ts.

*'We can experience this by watering the root of a tree—God. Love God and we automatically begin to love everyone.'*

Love is one of the words we use most and understand least. In this material world, the word 'love' has lost its meaning. A devotee realises the presence of God by loving Him unconditionally. We can call it a special kind of love—spiritual love. If we love God, we will gradually realise how much He loves us.

Krishna says:

*'If one offers me love and devotion, a leaf, a flower, a fruit or water, I will accept it.'*

The process of *attaining this* is very easy and anyone can attempt it, even the poorest of the poor.

God does not want any kind of special offerings. He does not need anything from anyone because He has everything, and He is self-sufficient. He accepts the offering of His *bhakt* in exchange of love and affection. The only qualification required in this connection is to be a pure devotee of the Lord. We cannot take *bhakti* casually. Without the basic principle of *nishkam bhakti*, nothing can impress God or make Him agree to accept anything from anyone. This process is eternal. If our *bhakti* is casual and we are a materialist, any number of offerings in the form of money or material will not be accepted by God.

The beauty of pure *bhakti* is that we can take as much as we are ready for.

Krishna says:

*'There is no loss in this endeavour.'*

Bring *bhakti* in life and see the benefits. God is great but *nishkam bhakti* is greater than God because it attracts Him.

How is it possible that one who is actually engaged in bhakti fails to become purified of sinful deeds or sinful activities? The answer is that *bhakti* has the power to actually remove all kinds of reactions to sinful deeds.

One who is engaged in *bhakti* has without doubt become freed from all impurities of materials and sinful activities. Krishna considers a true *bhakt* very deserving as to neutralise his sinful activities by becoming alert and avoiding to commit any sinful activities again.

As Krishna says:

*'Even if one commits the most abominable action, if he engages in* bhakti, *he is to be considered saintly, for he has rightly understood that there is nothing like devoted worship of God.'*

This means that sometimes a devotee commits some act which may be taken as unpleasant, hurtful or disgusting, socially and politically. Due to that sinful activity he falls in the eyes of the society, *but if his intentions are not bad* and he wholeheartedly engages himself in pure *bhakti*, then the God within his heart, purifies him and excuses him from that *unintentional sin*.

The impact of pure *bhakti* is so strong that such an occasional fall is at once rectified. No one should ridicule or make sarcastic comments on a devotee for some accidental fall. *The accidental fall of a devotee from the path of saintliness does not make him corrupt or bad forever.* Such occasional falls will stop in due course as a devotee is completely engaged in pure *bhakti*, which means he is saintly.

Krishna says:

*'Speedily such a person becomes virtuous and attains lasting peace. O son of Kunti, know it for sure, that my devotee never falls. Arjuna, declare boldly that my devotee never perishes.'*

This should not be misunderstood that a person engaged in sinful activities, either by accident or by intention, is not a devotee. His continuous remembrance of God and pure *bhakti* make him pure by nature. The purifying process is already there in the heart of the devotee, due to his constant remembering of the divine. His prayers should be continued without any break. This will protect the devotee from an accidental fall. He will remain free from all material contaminations.

*Bhaktiyoga* is a very simple way to reach ultimate oneness with God. Sincere and regular *bhakti* creates good *karma*, which brings happiness. It frees us from suffering by making us detached from the material world. The *bhakti marg* gives meaning to our life by removing all negativity from our inner system. It makes our heart pure and a temple of love and compassion. Pure *bhakti* can lessen the *karmic* effect and help in breaking the *karmic* chain. Through prayers we can quickly purify our negative *karma*. Unselfishness and generosity in *bhakti* make us wise and knowledgeable, thus removing ignorance and false belief about ourselves. We start sowing good *karmic* seeds that bear fruit in this life and beyond. We learn to examine ourselves first before criticising the actions of others.

A fool is one who keeps God last on his list. The person who keeps God first on his list is certainly a wise man because he has understood properly that he may accumulate any amount of wealth, but eventually death will snatch it away from him. So there is no sense in wasting time in accumulating things which will be snatched away in the end. This desire and attachment to the world make us postpone adoption of the *bhakti marg*. People don't want to give up anything until the last moment. When there is nothing left for us to do in this world or when people forcibly retire us, would it be time then for us to do *bhakti*? Now is the time. It is always *now*. There is no other way for time to come; it is always *now*.

When we become weak and old, when we walk with the help of a stick, would we be able to remember the divine then? For remembering the divine, we have to divert our entire energy towards Him and that can only be done when we are young and full of energy.

God is always there within us, but we keep running around everywhere. God is in our house, but we are never at home because we are busy chasing our dreams.

Now, if we decide to adopt the *bhakti marg*, many obstacles will come in this path in the form of money, power, name, fame. We have to free ourselves from worldly attachments, little by little. We have to be careful on this path. We have to become aware. If we are aware, then nobody can stop us. This awareness comes from a perfect combination of *bhakti* and *gyana*. This combination is the ultimate event. When this happens, there is nothing higher than this. When *bhakti* and *gyana* unite, where devotion is knowledge and knowledge is devotion, then that becomes the temple, the temple where God resides. There is no greater power than this. It needs our total dedication and our complete surrender to God.

We must awaken all our dormant energy as early as possible and we will notice *bhakti* happening within us without any effort. *Bhakti* happens without going to the temple. But

if we go on postponing it until tomorrow, that tomorrow will never come. This way it cannot work.

When we have energy, we are young, we do commit wrongs and when we don't have any energy, when we are about to die, we want to remember God. We use our youth to enjoy the worldly things and offer our old age to the Divine. We need a lot of energy and hard work to remember God or to pray.

The day we start this, we notice that we have that in us. We start growing and our smallness starts disappearing.

*Bhakti and gyana go hand in hand.*

*Bhakti* can impart meaningfulness in our life while knowledge can remove meaninglessness. Layers of ignorance and attachments collected within can be cleared by acquiring knowledge and *nishkam bhakti.* Then it is possible to do *sakshatkar* and see *parmatma.* When we have created space by decluttering ourselves through *gyana* and *bhakti*, God rushes towards us from all sides. If we are full of materialistic desires, then we are not leaving any space for God. We need to allow God to take care of us.

We don't need to say God aloud; the inner emotion is enough. When our heart is full of divine love and we are making no effort to do anything from our side, then it is time when God rushes towards you. We need to take a step towards God.

If we go on holding on to life, then we are depriving ourselves of *amrit*, the nectar. We will only see death. Nectar and death are hidden within us.

*Food for Thought*

- Every stage of inner growth means a good life because it is nurtured by God.
- God will help us to move ahead when it is time to move on.
- Many make fun of spirituality. Don't bother. Move on.

- Driven by ambition and haunted by guilt is more spiritual than pretending to be a saint.
- *Bhakti* and meditation will help us to be more open to love, compassion and wisdom.
- Difficult situations offer us a way to be spiritually strong by practising *bhakti*.
- Praying selflessly purifies the negative *karmas*.
- Prayers train the mind to think positively.

□

# Gyanayoga

*'Wisdom is awakening to the fact that there will always be something else to desire."*

## Gyanayoga

'*For* gyana, *the* Bhagvad Gita *is supposed to be practiced and not learnt.*'

It is beyond one's capacity to understand and explain the *Gita*. We have to become Arjuna, which means that we have to adopt the role of Arjuna to understand Krishna. We have to reach the peak level of '*vishada*' to understand the *Gita*. When Arjuna was depressed and full of '*vishada*', he told Krishna of his unwillingess to fight the battle. Krishna then explained to him the *sankhyayoga* followed by *karmayoga*. The reason was that without *gyana*, we will keep on doing the same *karma* again and again, thus getting trapped in the cycle of suffering. Unless we apply wisdom, we cannot understand the true meaning of *karmayoga*. The *Gita* explains the right meaning of the simple principles of life through *gyanayoga. Sankhyayoga* or *gyanayoga* constitute a great science.

This means wisdom, which in turn is the awakening of right understanding. Wisdom is one thing and knowledge is another. Knowledge, actually, is the accumulation of experiences and has continuity. Without continuity, there is no knowledge. Wisdom is when knowledge ends. Wisdom cannot be replaced by knowledge and no amount of explanation or accumulation of facts can free man from suffering. If the cause of suffering is not explained, then life becomes worthless, full of pain and miseries. Wisdom has nothing to do with logic, but has everything to do with knowing what is right and what is wrong. Knowing right or wrong is intelligence and intelligence is inborn. We are born with it.

Wisdom develops a psychological understanding of good and bad. If we are not wise, we can waste this life as well as many lives to come. The primary aim of any human being should be to lead his life and conduct his thinking and behaviour, in a world of conflicting truths, in such a way, so that he can overcome his sufferings and attain peace. The truth is that suffering is the central and dominant part of human life. It is further aggravated by transience and materialism and our inability to cope with it. Without providing satisfactory answers to the problem of suffering, no scripture, no *guru*, no belief system or religion can satisfy our intellectual need to find a solution. Suffering, therefore, is the first and most important mystery to be explored, understood and resolved before one can proceed safely and convincingly on the path of spirituality.

Nature has interwoven suffering into every aspect of human life, so that it serves as a grim reminder of our imperfections, incapacity and inadequacies. It is so deeply ingrained in our nature that it cannot be separated from us as long as we cling to our old ways.

Lord Krishna pointed to the unnecessary suffering borne by Arjuna. Krishna said that *Arjuna was speaking like a wise person, yet he was suffering like an ignorant person by grieving for those who did not deserve to be grieved.'* Arjuna's suffering was caused by ignorance and delusion or his mistaken notions about self. In ignorance we tend to take transient things as reality. Because of ignorance, the vision of greatness and nobility is absent because we are surrounded and dominated by temporary things. For this reason, it is difficult for human beings to stay calm and peaceful.

*'Your wisdom opens up the channels which are hidden by ignorance.' What is ignorance?*

## Ignorance

*'Ignorance is the ultimate source of all suffering.'*

A definition of 'ignorance' is lack of knowledge or information. Ignorance is also the refusal to learn and also the refusal to try and understand the viewpoints of others. Ignorance does not mean that we are foolish, but when we are ignorant and think that we are knowledgeable, then it is foolishness. Except for knowledge, no other exercise can remove wrong information or knowledge or *ignorance*. When there is right knowledge, ignorance disappears. The right knowledge removes the cause of wrong actions. As a diamond is cut by another diamond, only a logical analysis of right knowledge can remove ignorance or the wrong knowledge.

Ignorance is not absence of knowledge. If this was absence of knowledge, we could have borrowed knowledge. We can even steal knowledge, but borrowing or stealing cannot make us wise. We have to grow into it. Unless we grow into something, it is never ours. So, unless knowing takes place in our being, ignorance cannot be dissolved.

Ignorance is the root cause of all sufferings. An ignorant man believes that whatever wrong is happening to him is due to the supernatural power and events are decided in advance; so he has no control over them. To understand the truth behind it, we require wisdom, which tells us that we are responsible for our sufferings and the supernatural power has nothing to do with our sufferings.

How can we know or recognise an ignorant person?

When there is no illumination, no light, no knowledge, then that is a sign of an ignorant person. An ignorant person acts whimsically for no purpose. Even though he has the capacity to work, he makes no effort. He is in a state of illusion. Though consciousness is there, life is inactive. These are symptoms of one who is in the mode of ignorance.

Ignorance is filled with knowing. The more ignorant we

are, the more we will think that we know all. The main reason for ignorance is our false ego, a false belief or impression about ourselves. *Ignorance is 'I am', which means, 'I am the doer. I'm the enjoyer. The world revolves around me.'* If we are so self-obsessed, it is hard to get rid of ignorance because we have so many masks of *kama, vaasna, moha* and more than that, our false ego is very strong and powerful. Ignorance means foolishness, while foolishness means unconsciousness, living in sleep and not being awake.

If we really want to get rid of our ignorance, wisdom (*gyana)* is the only remedy for our problem. If we want to free ourselves from the shackles of ignorance, *gyana* is very essential. Nobody can be free without *gyana. Gyana* is knowing the difference between right and wrong. Except for right knowledge, no other exercise can remove the wrong knowledge or ignorance. This right 'knowing' does not happen by collecting information, going to any *guru* or attending a *satsang*. Knowledge does not mean knowledge of scriptures as it is not so very important. Knowing the difference between right and wrong can never be a borrowed phenomenon. If we wish to know something, we have to know it ourselves; others cannot make us know it. Only we can know and nobody else can know it for us. *Gurus*, teachers and scriptures are just there as aids to help us to know the right path. We have to put in our own efforts to reach this 'knowing'.

In spiritual tradition, knowledge was passed on from one person to another as is evident from the *Upanishads.* In spiritual terms, what matter is 'knowing', which is more intuitive. In Indian philosophy and scriptures, knowledge is identified as '*avidya*'.

***Avidya*** (worldly knowledge)

Knowledge can be destroyed or contrary arguments can be given about our worldly knowledge. An intelligent person cares much more for the capacity to know, to learn. His genuine interest is in knowing, not in knowledge. Though knowledge makes our memory bigger and better, but our intelligence does not become bigger and better. When we are not dependent on books for knowledge, this makes us intelligent in some difficult matters because then we use our mind.

***Vidya*** (spiritual understanding)

Knowledge can be destroyed, but there is no way that our understanding can be taken away. *Vidya* is understanding. No logic can destroy our understanding. Understanding is like a tree, whose roots reach deep into the earth and find the hidden source of water. Such a tree can live on its own; it is not dependent on others.

***Pragya*** (intelligence)

Intelligence is beyond worldly knowledge and spiritual understanding. *Pragya* is 'knowing' and this 'knowing' is part of growth. In *pragya,* memorising of the *Gita* is not very important. Understanding the *Gita* is important. Applying the theory of *Gita* practically on ourselves is important.

Ignorance is our ego, which can exist only with knowledge because you can say, 'I know'. The emphasis obviously is not on knowing; the emphasis is on 'I'. But when we say, 'I don't know', the emphasis is not on ignorance, but is on egolessness. This makes us wiser. The wiser we become, the more aware and understanding we become, the more we feel how ignorant we are, or we were. A moment comes when we feel that we don't know anything. When one feels that one does not know anything, the ego disappears. That is why it is said that ultimate knowledge is hidden within. Only the ignorant, who has no experience, no inner realisation, depends on the outer knowledge. One who is full of *avidya*, ignorance, does not look within to find happiness; instead he goes out in search of happiness.

The state of ignorance is the cause of all delusions, of all unrealities, of all false appearances. But to know more is not the state of knowledge. Ignorance is the cause, but knowledge is not the remedy. We can know more and more and more, but we still remain the same. Knowledge becomes addiction. We go on adding to it, but the person who is trying to attain knowledge remains the same. Worldly knowledge is there, but we are not wise. Undoubtedly, the root cause of all our misery is ignorance, but this type of knowledge is not the remedy.

**Awakening is the remedy.**

If we don't understand this simple difference, first we would be considered to be lost in ignorance, and then we will be lost in knowledge.

According to the *Upanishads*, in ignorance, people are lost, but in knowledge, they are lost in a deeper manner. So, unless 'knowing' happens in our being, ignorance cannot be removed. Ignorance is not absence of knowledge; ignorance is absence of 'awareness'. Ignorance is a state of sleep as if we are doing things in sleep. In such a state, we are not aware of what we are doing.

Krishna says:

*'The one who is ignorant, who does not have trust and who is sceptic, perishes. 'To show them special mercy, I, dwelling in their hearts, destroy with the shining lamp of knowledge, the darkness born of ignorance.'*

*'Ignorance is our greatest enemy. 'Battle the universal enemy of ignorance with* gyana.'

Ignorance is the main cause of all our sinful activities. Ignorance is the reason for a sinful life and a sinful life is the cause of one living on in material existence. An abnormal birth is a very serious introspective matter. An abnormal person suffers the present life due to the results of sinful activities committed in his past life. If he still leads a sinful life by not correcting his *karmas*, it means that he is creating further suffering in his future life.

What is a sin?

## Sin

*'Ignorance is sin and awareness is virtue'*

An immoral act considered to be transgression against divine law is a sin. An action that is felt to be highly reprehensible is a sin. A sin is something which is difficult to remove from our inner slate. Even a single sin against God's law is enough to deserve eternal damnation. The sin of the father carry on to the third or fourth generation.

A sin is not an action; it is a consequence. Killing by a doctor in a hospital becomes a good action if the patient suffers from a terminal illness and cannot be revived, while killing by a criminal becomes a crime and a sin. A sin is a state of acting without being in total control of oneself because no man in his right state of mind will ever do anything sinful. The act can become a sin only because the doer is ignorant or in a subconscious state of mind. We can commit a sin, we can repent a sin, we can replace a sin by a virtuous act, but it will not be of any use according to the *Upanishads*, if we remain the same. Unless we change for the better or our consciousness changes, merely a change of an act is useless. The basic requirement for committing a sin is to be in an unconscious state of mind. The more we are alert, conscious and aware, the less is the possibility of committing a sin. In a fully aware person, the thought of a sin cannot arise just as in a fully lit room, darkness cannot exist.

We cannot fight darkness because darkness means the absence of light. Bring in the light and darkness disappears. The *Upanishads* say that a *sin* is darkness and once you bring in the light of consciousness, the sin disappears. As alertness grows 'within' and the sin disappears 'without'.

This awareness and consciousness tells us how *prakriti* (nature) functions within a person. Understanding this *prakriti* is a high standpoint for looking at things. The entire humanity has been conditioned to believe that man is a sinner because they are unable to understand that he commits a sin when forced by the *triguna* (*prakriti*). No amount of punishment will change a man till he understands that he is forced to commit a sin because of his *prakriti* or the *triguna* which are *sattva, rajasa* and *tamasa.* Everything around us can be categorised as *sattvic, rajasic* and *tamasic,* depending on the predominant component we are made up of. In other words, every human being's mind is made of a mixture of these three basic traits present in different proportions.

*Sattva* teaches us compassion, truthfulness and devotion to God while leading us to wisdom, consciousness and alertness. To lead a sin-free life, we need to imbibe the *sattvic* way of life. The philosophy of *Bhagvad Gita* is that *sankhya,* which means *gyana,* tells us that all activity belongs to *prakriti*;only consciousness belongs to us. Whatever virtuous or sinful life we lead is due to *prakriti*; only awareness belongs to us. If we attain awareness, all sins can be destroyed and we would be united with Parbrahman.

The *Upanishads* say that when we are awake and alert, only then we realise that it was *prakriti* which was doing all. We have always been a witness—*the purusha* (*atman*).

We cannot fight with sin nor can we think in terms of sin, else we will feel guilty and it will retard our spiritual growth; rather it would be our fall.

If we keep committing sins, it shows only one thing—that we are fast asleep and unaware. We should not fight with the sin; rather, on the contrary, move 'within' and become more alert. If we are concerned with the sin as an act, it makes us suffer from guilt and we cannot feel the divine because our guilt becomes a barrier. The gratitude cannot exist there. When we feel that a centre exists within, then we draw nearer and nearer to awareness and become more and more grateful. If something is wrong with our consciousness, our act will go wrong. If our conscious is right, our acts will follow.

The *Upanishads* say that sin is like darkness. We cannot fight darkness, because darkness means absence of light. When we bring the light of consciousness, then darkness in the form of sin disappears.

A moment comes when we are simply a flame of light within, alert to whatsoever we do, alert to whatsoever happens within us. There is no sin then. The more we try to be conscious, the more we feel that God has some destiny to fulfil. This process is scientific and yet spiritual, because it gives us dignity.

The *'sutra'* says that one who realises *'self'*, he destroys the sin. Just by realising the Parbrahman, sins are destroyed, even our past sins. Just by reaching and touching the inner self our accumulated wrong deeds and sins get destroyed. We have passed them; we have gone beyond them. We may think that we are not doing anything to destroy our sins, then how can they be destroyed?

The *Upanishads* say that when a person is awake, self-realised and has touched Brahman, then all his bad deeds and sins disappear like a long dream. With a new awareness, all that is past becomes illusory or as if it had never happened.

That is why the *Upanishads* call this world *maya,* an illusion. Once we realise our sinful actions, sinful deeds, we can stop committing any more as this understanding marks the beginning of *gyana*. This *gyana* alone can help us fight the toughest of battles in the world. *Gyana* alone can make us understand that we are unable to lead a normal life due to our past sinful life. As soon as we realise this, we start making efforts so that we don't face a similar situation in the next birth. As the blazing fire can burn any amount of fuel to ashes, similarly *gyana-agni* can burn all the fuel of sinful activities. A *gyani* is always alert and tries not to commit any sinful activity. But ignorance is no excuse for escaping the reaction, that is, the distress. Sinful activities are like seeds, which are of two types: those which can sprout and those which cannot. The sinful activities for which we suffer at the present moment are like sprouted seeds. The many sinful activities lying dormant within us for which we have not yet suffered are considered as unsprouted seeds. They will sprout in the future or may be in the next birth. In this way, a chain of sinful activities occur and are naturally connected to distress. We therefore suffer life after life due to these sins.

- Ingratitude is the biggest sin for which there is no forgiveness.
- A sin cannot be understood until we understand our inner 'self'.
- A sin leaves an impression, while wrong deeds are generally forgotten.

In the following pages, lets explore some important factors, Spiritual and Practical Wisdom rides and relies on.

## Types of *Karma*

The meaning of wisdom is difficult to pin down. When we talk of wisdom, we do not speak merely of amassing information, or even practical knowhow, although both knowledge and knowhow are frequently described as an important aspect of wisdom. Wisdom is a way of knowing rather than possessing it. It is a quest for truth which involves knowledge over ignorance and insight over illusion, be it about the nature of the Universe, or the meaning of our lives. For spirituality, knowledge is not enough; we need *gyana* or wisdom because the more ignorant we are, the more we will think that we know all. We think that since we have read so many books, scriptures, we are knowledgeable. Knowledge does not exist in books and scriptures; knowledge is a very personal thing. It is not an object to possess, a property, a wealth to own. If we think this, then we are an *agyani*.

The root cause of our suffering is *avidya*. We are ignorant about our real identity and keep on accumulating bad *karmic* seeds by getting attached to the pleasures attained through our senses. These seeds are unmanifest (*aprarabdha)* in the beginning, but if we keep on collecting these seeds, they turn into *prarabdha,* that is, they manifest as suffering not only in this life but even in the next births too.

It is very important to understand that *karma* is of three kinds:

1. *Sanchita*
2. *Prarabdha*
3. *Kriyamana*

***Sanchita:*** *Sanchita* means the accumulated *karma* of the past. A part of it is seen in the character of the man, in his tendencies, aptitudes, capacities, inclinations and desires, etc.

*Sanchita* is we pay our debts.

***Prarabdha:*** *Prarabdha* is part of *sanchita karma,* a collection of past *karmas,* which are ready to be experienced through the present body. *Prarabdha* is that portion of past *karma* which is responsible for the present body. *Sanchita karma,* which influences human life in the present birth, is called *prarabdha.*

*It is ripe for reaping.* It cannot be avoided or changed. *Prarabdha karma* is that which has begun and is actually bearing fruit. *We pay for our past debts.*

***Kriyamana:*** *Kriyamana* is that *karma,* which is being prepared for the future. It is also called *agami or vartaman.*

In Vedic literature, it is explained beautifully. *Tarkash* (quiver) is *sanchita karma.* The arrow that is ready for shooting represents *kriyamana* and the arrow which has left the bow, which cannot return back, is *prarabdha.*

The whole lot of *sanchit karma* is destroyed by attaining knowledge of Brahman or the eternal. *Agami karma* can be destroyed by *prayaschita*—purification, regret and repentance.

*Prarabdha* can only be overcome by the grace of the Lord. His Grace is all powerful. The law of nature does not operate when there is grace of the Almighty. We have an example of Markandeya, who conquered death by *purushartha.* By sincere and intense *purushartha* (intense efforts), *prarabdha* can be changed. If we have faith in God, everything is possible.

We can destroy any bad *karma* we want to so long as we remember that bad *karma* in this birth grows into a big tree and the deed is again repeated.

With the help of wisdom, we can start realising our bad actions on some occasions and on certain situations as we know by now what do *sanchit, kriyaman* and *prarabdha karma* mean. With the help of *gyana*, we accept the full responsibility. This creates regret and repentance in us and we try to do things and behave in a positive manner. At this stage, some wrong committed in the past, haunts our consciousness. Wisdom makes us conscious, pure and positive, which purify our soul by clearing all the negative *karma.* It makes us guilt-free and comfortable with ourselves. We feel quite different and positive all the time. If we don't purify our negative *karma* in this birth, then we carry them to the next birth.

We cannot prevent the adverse to happen, but, through *gyana* we can change the unfortunate circumstances. We can change our response by practicing moral restraint and patience. Wisdom can show us the path to resolve the adverse circumstances. Patience is the wise response in the face of adversity as it lessens our sufferings.

Purification, regret and repentance can transform our bad deeds, and this can only be done through wisdom (*gyana*). *Gyana* tells us the do's and don'ts, and if we follow these, slowly but surely we will be able to purify our soul. The fire of wisdom burns all the effects of our past and present bad *karma.*

Wisdom is the ability to think and act by using knowledge,

understanding, common sense and insight. Wisdom is when we understand that this phenomenal world, or the material world in which we are placed, is complete in itself because of twenty-four elements, of which this material universe is a temporary manifestation and which are necessary for the maintenance and subsistence of this universe.

## Twenty-four Elements

According to the *sankhya* philosophy of the *Gita*:

This material world works through the conjunctions of the soul and the twenty-four material elements.

The twenty-four elements are:

- Five great elements (*mahabhutas):* Earth, water, fire, air and ether (empty space).
- Five knowledge-acquiring senses *(gyanendriyas)*: Eyes, nose, ear, tongue (mouth), skin.
- Five subtle elements (the objects known by the *gyanendriyas*): Sight, smell, sound, taste, touch.
- Five working senses: Hands, legs, mouth, rectum, genitals.
- Four subtle (invisible) elements: Mind, intelligence, ego and the unmanifested stage of the three modes of *prakriti* (nature).

Thus, there are 24 material elements that constitute all material creations and the bodies.

The material world which is the field for activities is nature and the enjoyer of nature is the living entity, and above both is the Supreme Controller, the *paramatma*, God.

The embodied soul is trapped by the body, which is a casing, a covering, made up of the twenty-four elements and the *process* of knowledge. Those who try to understand *this* by cultivation of knowledge are able to understand the twenty-four elements. They understand that the individual soul is transcendental to the material elements and through *gyana*, they are able to understand that above the individual soul is present the supreme soul, the *paramatma.*

Wisdom is when you know that 'self' (soul) is in fact neither a doer nor an enjoyer. It is *prakriti (triguna)* that acts as such. He, who thinks that *'prakriti does everything and I am only a witness, a non-doer, a non-enjoyer,'* is a wise person.

No amount of protest on the part of a being can stop *prakriti* from functioning. We can only be a silent witness of the action of *prakriti.*

What is *triguna?*

## Prakriti Triguna

*'Material nature consists of three modes—goodness, passion and Ignorance.'* Guna literally means property or quality. *Triguna* means three qualities comprising *sattva, rajas* and *tamas.* The subtle basic components *(trigunas)* are the fabric of creation. They permeate through all living and non-living, tangible and intangible, things.

Krishna says:

*'Every being under* prakriti *is made up of the trigunas known as* sattva, rajas *and* tamas. Sattva *is purity and holiness,* rajas *is to do action and drive and* tamas *is laziness and inertia.'*

All words, actions, temperaments, aspirations, conduct and character of every individual are reflected by the proportions in which these three qualities exist in the mind. *Trigunas* also influence the behaviour of all things, depending on which one of the three subtle components is predominant within us. It influences our reactions to situations.

Since they are not physical in nature, it is difficult to spot them and give them a physical characteristic. These three subtle basic components can only be perceived by the subtle sense organs or our sixth sense.

The *gunas* are born from *prakriti.* In any human being, though all these three qualities will be present in varying proportions, generally one of these qualities will be more predominant than the other two. Every human being takes birth in this world and engages in action, deeds, *karmas*. When the soul takes birth, its psyche is built essentially with an appropriate mix of *trigunas* based on the *karma* of its previous birth. In spiritual life, knowledge of *triguna* is imperative. A correct understanding of the three qualities of *prakriti* is essential to overcome our bondage to earthly life and attain liberation.

*Sattva* is purity and knowledge.

*Sattva* binds the soul through detachment with happiness and knowledge. *Sattva* is love, compassion, devotion to God (*bhakti),* truthfulness, *viveka* (wisdom*), vairagya (*dispassion), *tyag* (sacrifice), detachment, kindness, control over senses, non-jealousy, honesty, patience, mercy and humility.

*Rajas* is action and drive.

*Rajas* is born out of *trishna* (thirst for intense desire) and is full of passion and attachment.

*Rajas* is activeness, impatience, ambition, passion, motivation, power, manipulation, desire for leadership, domination, self-promotion, rule breaking, pushy, love for subjugating others, love for grandeur, competitive instinct, workaholism, exhibitionism, strenuous effort, materialism, avarice, authoritativeness and pride.

*Tamas* means laziness, inertia, darkness, ignorance.

*Tamas* is dullness, sloth, greed without putting an effort, lack of motivation, negativism, excess sleep, jealousy, envy, miserliness, pessimism, perverted desires, hatred, lust, vengeance, daydreaming, treachery, possessiveness, aversion, rumour mongering, backbiting, dishonesty, laxity.

In short, *sattva* shows the way to reach God.

*Rajas* binds the soul with attachment through action.

*Tamas* is darkness. It is born out of ignorance and *moha* or delusion. It binds the soul with recklessness, indolence and sleep.

No two individuals' conduct, character, aspirations, values are same because the ratio in which these *trigunas* are present in the psyche of each person is different.

Krishna says:

*'When all the gates of the human body are illuminated by knowledge, it means* sattva *is predominant. When* rajas *is predominant, greed, worldliness, a penchant for selfish activities arise. With the increase of* tamas, *one can see the flourishing of darkness, inactivity and delusion.'*

Whether it is *sattva, rajas, or tamas,* the *trigunas* are a part of *prakriti* and responsible for our ignorance, bondage, delusion and sufferings on earth. We cannot be free until they are fully resolved.

'Kaliyuga *is where* tamas *and* rajas *are predominant*.'

By knowing the distinction among three *gunas* and by developing the quality and mode of *sattva* in abundance, a person can purify his mind and body and experience peace and equanimity. A person can increase the *sattva guna* by following desireless actions, selfless service, *bhakti,* self-realisation, *sattvic* knowledge, *sattvic* behaviour and even the food which we eat is important. *Sattvic* food cultivates *sattvic* behaviour.

*'God can be attained through* sattva guna. Rajas *and* tamas *separate us from God.'*

Krishna says:

*'When one properly sees that in all the activities, no other performer is at work than* triguna, *he knows the Supreme Lord, who is transcendental to all these modes. He attains a spiritual nature.'*

The *Gita* tells us that we should become wiser and strive to transcend the *gunas* rather than cultivate them. Once *sattva* is present in full measure, there won't be much of delay to do *sakshatkar* (God's vision). A little more progress will make a *sattvic* person attain God. But for that, one should go beyond the *trigunas* to attain immortality and freedom from birth, death, old age and sorrow.

When we are able to transcend the *trigunas*, we can enjoy nectar even in this life, which is the state of ultimate happiness.

One cannot attain the knowledge of *Parabrahman* without transcending the *trigunas*. Touching Brahman is the constitutional position of ultimate happiness.

So, now, we are able to understand that everyone is under the influence of *triguna* and works according to *prakriti's* three modes—the *sattva-rajas-tamas gunas*, which unless one tries to transcend them, wanders perpetually within the cycle of birth and death. This knowledge of *Gita* constitutes a great science, and each and every living being has to understand it for his own interest.

## Attachment

Our attachments aim to perpetuate our individual and collective identities, egos, interests and values. Attachments are responsible for our cravings and the compulsive need to accumulate, in order to feel complete, fulfilled and secure. When we are subject to attachments, we react differently to different situations. We suffer from conflicting emotions. We live with the fear of loss or the hope of gain. We become defensive or aggressive. We take positions. We change positions. We criticise, we admire, we become vulnerable, manipulative, selfish and self-centred. Our attachments prevent us from being who we are and what we can be. They do not let us experience reality without influencing our understanding. They hold us back from flowing with life. We become limited and self-centred because of our attachments. We wear masks and pretend what we are not. We lose touch with the reality. Attachment is therefore a fundamental problem, which can be resolved only by cultivating *non-attachment*.

To be free from attachments, we must be willing to let go of everything, renounce our attachment to things and embrace change. To be free from attachments does not mean that we have stopped being happy or turned ourselves away from all the positive things in life. Non-attachment does not mean we should not have the zest for life.

So, what is non-attachment/detachment?

## Detachment

*'Attachment and suffering go hand in hand. Desire is the cause; attachment is the result.'* When the mind is constantly engaged in worldly things, it grows fond of them and develops attachment. Attachment is the desire to hold on to a permanent state, or a desire to keep a thing or a person permanently. Attachment generates craving, wanting and insecurity which constitute the main cause for suffering. Nothing else can be so poisonous as attachment or so-called possessiveness. Attachment takes us away from our real being as we become focused on the things to which we are attached. Not only people become attached to physical objects or things, but also to relationships, ideas, opinions, success and failure. Attachment is when we think that if we obtain all the things that we desire, we can be happy. However, the reality is opposite. Attachment towards materialism can create anxiety, fear, anger, jealousy, hopelessness, sadness, pride or vanity. We will notice that a negative emotion arises, which is because we are attached to something and are unable to hold it.

Attachment turns into bondage and slavery. We become a slave of our attachment. Attachment is the main inability to practice detachment and the lack of attachment is detachment.

Krishna says:

*'When you are neither clinging to a thing nor running away from it, when you become receptive to everything—good or bad, beautiful or ugly, pleasant or painful—then your mind*

*remains unscathed and unmarked. And such a mind is a non-attached mind.'*

A non-attached mind, according to Krishna, is one which accepts everything unconditionally.

Practicing detachment in no way implies renouncing family life or being emotionally or physically unavailable. Detachment is not really about disengaging ourselves from our families, friends, possessions and passions. Also, non-attachment does not mean avoiding empathy, or being a less compassionate person. We can be detached but at the same time we are affectionate. Attachment and affection are two different things. Attachment makes us manipulative and weak, while affection means that there is a healthy emotional give and take between the two people in the relationship. Affection is the natural part of human existence and spiritual existence, while attachment hold us back.

Some people think that detachment is negative, as it takes us away from life enjoyment (materialism). In fact, non-attachment is one of the most misunderstood words. True detachment is not separation from life, but it gives us absolute freedom within our mind to explore things and actually provides several benefits to everyone.

*'Detachment is not synonymous with indifference, carelessness.'* Detachment is not hard-heartedness; it's level-headedness. We need to act with detachment, doing the right thing for its own sake without worrying about success or failure. Sometimes there are certain relationships that are injurious, or abusive, or may be harmful and at that stage, detachment enables us to step back and step away from such situations, relationships and actions which are harmful to us. So, in that sense, detachment is a source of strength. Here, detachment does not mean hard-heartedness, but being level-headed.

We have to pay attention to our attachment and neutralise it so that it will not trouble us by its presence or absence. Emotional detachment can be a positive behaviour which allows a person to react calmly to highly emotional circumstances. It is a deliberate mental attitude which avoids engaging in emotions of others. It does not mean avoiding empathy, but to achieve the space to choose whether or not to be overwhelmed or manipulative in certain situations.

**How to attain detachment?**

We are ordinary until we attain non-attachment.

*'An ordinary person is one who is attached. Extraordinary comes with non-attachment.'*

An attached person cannot think of himself without money and the detached cannot think of himself in association with money. Detachment is a state in which a person overcomes his or her attachment to desires for material things, people or concepts and thus attains a heightened perspective.

Our religious knowledge by itself does not guarantee freedom from desires and attachments. What liberates us is freedom from desires and attachments. The solution for this is to increase *sattva* (purity). When *sattva* is predominant, people are attached to virtue. When *sattva* is in abundance, then awareness can turn inwards because we don't have anything outside to catch hold of. *Sattva* brings non-attachment within us. We don't have to practice non- attachment because non-attachment is our nature. We are born with it.

If it is the power of our personal desire that keeps us bound to the earth, it is same as power, when harnessed, will take us to a higher consciousness. And that power is detachment; the art of withdrawing desire from lesser things; meaningless attachments.

Detachment is a bliss which is hidden in the very depths of our hearts. When we grow in detachment, we will grow healthier, happier. Detachment is not only pure Bliss; it is also the secret of our good health. A mind at peace and a heart flooded with love can release powers that strengthen our physical system. Detachment is a longevity skill. Freedom from attachments, emotional entanglements, is a sure shot way to remove depression, anxiety and mental illness.

Detachment does not imply running away from the world, but it is living free from the shackles of the world and the attractions and distractions it has to offer.

Krishna says:

*'While living in the world, live like a lotus flower.'*

The lotus is born in dirty and stagnant water, lives in water, yet remains untouched or polluted by it.

By turning inwards, one attains non-attachment. This helps in deep involvement with life. We can know ourself, when we recognise that the only genuine source of happiness is living as our true self. When we think this way, then such a mind is a non-attached mind. We have understood detachment. We have understood 'bliss and joy'.

If we want to judge whether we are detached or not, joy is the criterion of our detachment.

*'Non-attachment is the secret of finding oneself.'* Now, we have learnt the art of detachment. Once we are detached, we feel that being revengeful towards anybody is like being revengeful towards God. We accept the person for what he or she is; we still love him or her the way he or she is. Real forgiveness has no judgement. The more we forgive, the more we start moving towards God; forgiveness transcends us. By loving unconditionally and forgiving unconditionally, we will not accumulate any *karma*. We will not accumulate any past. Once we start forgiving, the distinction between a sinner and saint is lost. To forgive is to rise high. So, let this quality of forgiveness become our very pivot.

The quality and capacity to forgive is one of the most beautiful flowers of the human soul, while revenge is ugly. By forgiving, we experience something which is impossible to explain. It can only be called divine!

What is forgiveness?

## Forgiveness

*'Unforgiveness stands between us and God.'* Forgiveness is the intentional and voluntary process by which a victim undergoes a change in feelings and attitude regarding an offence. He or she lets go of negative emotions, such as revenge. When we hold on to hurt, pain, resentment and anger, it harms us more than it harms the offender. Forgiveness frees us to live in the present and allows us to move on without anger. Forgiveness is very important to our physical and mental health. This is for our own growth and happiness because if we don't forgive, we face chaos in our mind and life. Forgiveness frees us to live in the present.

Forgiveness is a conscious, deliberate decision to release feelings of resentment towards a person who has harmed us, regardless of whether they actually deserve our forgiveness or not. If someone has done wrong in the family, we have to forgive that person because if we don't support that person, if we don't forgive that person, we make a mess of our life.

Forgiveness does not mean forgetting, nor does it mean excusing offence made by the family member. It just means that we have made peace with the pain. Forgiveness should come from the bottom of our heart. We should support that member of our family and avoid gossiping about him. Neither should we discuss about our forgiveness. If others make fun of our forgiveness, don't bother.

If we are a parent, we can provide a wonderful model to our children and our forgiveness can be a gift to ourselves and our children.

Not forgiving is a form of punishment for ourself as well as for the offender. When the one we believe caused us harm is unwilling to take responsibility for his actions or insists that he did nothing wrong, it becomes even more necessary to forgive him because our non-forgiveness continues to prove the other wrong. Forgiveness is a more deliberate process that requires effort and practice. For this we can learn the art of 'stop telling ourselves' over and over again the story of what happened, how we were subjected to hurt and all the rest of upsetting words.

We don't need to be God while practicing forgiveness because forgetting is by no means an inherent part of forgiving. Forgiveness involves being willing and able to respond to what's happening in the present and not reacting to the incidents of past.

Forgiveness will release us from our past sin, due to which we have faced the situation. If we forgive, we clean the slate of past *karmic* sins. It is an act of self-realisation. This is our *nishkam karma*. We should repose faith in God's reward and punishment.

Those who have the nature of not forgiving others bring about bitterness, and this is linked to stress-related illnesses. By forgiving others, we free ourselves spiritually and emotionally. Trusting God's justice as God's timing is always the right time for each individual.

Forgiveness is ultimately about choosing love and with it comes happiness; it also means freedom from the shackles of anger, resentment and miseries.

## Money

We are ignorant about our real identity. Because of this ignorance, we keep on accumulating our sufferings. Sufferings are same whether we are rich or poor. When illness comes, it does not see whether we are rich or poor. Experience of pain during childbirth is same for a poor woman as well as for a rich woman. No amount of money or richness can protect us from depression, from physical and mental suffering or from serious illnesses. So, amassing wealth through wrong means is of no use if it is unable to protect us at the time of crises.

Money is worth nothing until we attach value to it. The

value of money is what we decide it to be its worth. So, it is possible for money to be valueless. If money is not able to protect us from suffering from unhappiness, it is of no use.

We do not have to possess money to pursue happiness. Happiness can be achieved in ways that do not require money. People were happy before money was invented, so happiness can come without it. Though money allows us to get things we want, but it cannot buy everything and certainly not happiness. Happiness, satisfaction and mental peace are few of the things which money cannot afford.

Most of the people are of the opinion that 'money is power'. It can make everything possible; even it can make an impossible possible.

But how much is enough? There is no limit to need. *Give me more* is a never-ending demand, which makes people very unhappy.

Can money buy happiness? There is no simple answer. Money can buy some happiness, but there is a real danger that extra money can actually make us miserable, that is, if our desire to spend grows with it. Finding a balance between having too little and having too much is not an easy task. Studies show that people who are materialistic tend to be less happy than those who are spiritual. Money cannot make a materialist happy because increased wealth brings increased expectations. We will never be content. If we are rich, but are not happy, what good is our money?

There is no harm in earning money as per one's capacity and need. Earning money is a duty for the family man. Money can help us to achieve our goals, but merely having money does not guarantee fulfilment. A balanced life is a fulfilling life. Once we define that so far is enough, we gain a sense of freedom. We are no longer caught up in the rat race and have time to pursue our passions. Other's money does not disturb our peace of mind and does not make us a money-earning machine. Life is short and hence time is precious. Enjoy every moment of life to its fullest with all the resources. We can use our money to save for things that truly matter.

We don't want to be rich, but we want to be happy. Real happiness comes from intentional activity, that is, the things we choose to do. Intentional activity happens when we act by doing things, like pursuing meaningful goals. It makes more sense to attain happiness through intentional activity which is by controlling things that we can and ignoring those we can't. Spiritual people believe that it is more important not to spend the entire life on making money rather than enjoying money. Materialism makes us less happy.

Richness means life well lived and is rich in security, relationships, experience. To improve our relationship with money, we must spend on the things that make us happiest, like going out on vacations, on *teertha yatras* that provide happiness and add some meaning to life.

Don't spend money on possessions as we tend start craving for the next big possession. Money makes us materialistic, leading us to miss out on life's simple pleasures.

**Money—The Spiritual Way**

*'The art of giving—be generous.'*

Money may mean different things for different people, but in its most basic form, it is a tool to enable and sustain a more comfortable life. It can free us from the stresses and obligations that people with lesser income have to deal with. Money is neither good nor bad but what we do with money is the important part. We are often so busy making money that we forget to spare a minute and think about what it means to us.

Money in itself is not happiness nor is true wealth. It is the basic requirement of life without which one cannot imagine a healthy and comfortable life. There is no doubt that money has the potential and capability to buy anything virtually and helps us throughout life. In this materialistic world, money is very important and a powerful tool without which one cannot live and survive. Though money is not everything in life, but it can be useful tool to achieve what we want in life, be it status, quality, convenience, time or even life.

For some, money is a great power—the power to choose one's own fate, power to tell others what to do, power to dictate your terms and condition. In *kaliyuga,* just to maintain their monetary status, people resort to corruption, bribe, smuggling, murder and other callous activities by degrading the moral and ethical values of humanity. Corrupt people follow wrong ways to earn money as they understand that the ways are simple and easy; however, this is not true. One can earn money in less time and effort but not for long, because soon he would be lost in the near future for adopting wrong methods. Such people can even forget their family, their moral values because their aim is to earn money and more money by any means whatsoever. They forget that no amount of money is going to prevent them from their sufferings, from diseases or mental illness, although money may make treatment of these ailments quicker and more easy. Accumulating money by wrong means is the biggest deception. We may be rich from outside, but we remain poor within. We have to put in more effort to maintain the status which we have earned by accumulating money. We live in constant fear of losing whatever we have. Though we have plenty of money, but we are not spending. We are not enjoying because we are worried about losing it all the time.

Money is not everything as it cannot buy things like time, love and true care. It can only fulfil the superficial needs of the person but not the spiritual needs, like true love. Money cannot give us security as it may not be there the next day. So, money and security are not the same thing. We can lose everything overnight, if that is our *karamphal*. Security can only come from within; it is an internal feeling. Materialism cannot give us security; it can only give momentary pleasure. Money is only good as the value it can add to our life; otherwise it is worthless. After a certain point, anything more than required is simply greed and avarice. To me personally, always thinking about money is merely a means to an end—the end being an ideal and peaceful life. Anything more than what is required to fund my ideal life is useless to me. I cannot take money or any material thing with me when I die. We take our good deeds with us, not our earthly deeds. We realise this only with God's blessings.

People who earn money by following ethical rules of humanity earn less money but for a long time and acquire a high status in society. Someone is ready to do anything to get money and for someone money is far from the list of important things and the latter are not poor. Rich people in the true sense do not possess money; they redirect money, they do philanthropy and the latter is true wealth. They will never put money as the centre of their life; for them money is the root of all evils.

Being a miser is the worst *karma* a person can do. God has punished us by making us a miser. We have plenty of money but no heart to spend as we are a born miser. This is the worst kind of punishment. We are tied to this *karma*. We are not spending. We are afraid of losing it, so we are always guarding it. It means money does not give us freedom; it gives us *bandhan*. We are always attached to it.

Attachment keeps us in this material world only. We can never think about freedom *moksha.* For *moksha,* we need to be generous and for being generous, we need to learn the art of giving. Be fearless! Fearlessness is the secret to security and Joy. Everything is going to remain here only. We are not taking anything with us. We came empty handed; will go empty handed. When we apply this to our lives, we become fearless and we know we are never alone on this path. God is with us and He is protecting us. We are sure nothing wrong will happen to us.

Lot of times, people try to be happy in the wrong ways—with money, with power, or with different things. Many persons have a wrong idea of what constitutes true happiness. In the following pages we will discover what happiness is.

## Happiness

Happiness is a feeling of contentment. Happiness is when our life fulfils our needs. Rarely can we find a human being who is not miserable. The misery is such, and they are entangled into it so deeply, that they don't see that any escape is possible. We can bring misery from the past. Someone might have insulted us yesterday and we may still be carrying the wound. We can still feel unhappy about it. Tomorrow our money will be finished, then where are we going to stay? Where will we eat? Unhappiness enters us, either it comes from yesterday, or it comes from tomorrow. But it is never here, now. The moment we desire happiness, we move away from the present. We have already moved into the future, which is nowhere.

Actually happiness has nothing to do what we have or don't have. However many things we may collect but perhaps they may increase our worries, our troubles, but happiness will not increase because of them. Certainly, unhappiness will increase with them because materialistic things have no relation to an increase in happiness. Worldly people are on the lookout for their happiness. For them happiness is outside. Even if they want to see God, they search God outside. They are under the false notion that they are enjoying the world. They say that they have all the worldly pleasures, so they are happy, but in reality, they are living in an illusion and actually suffering.

We should not be too concerned about money because

it is the greatest distraction against happiness. People think they will be happy if they have plenty of money, but money has nothing to do with happiness. I'm not against money; don't misinterpret me. Money is a means.

If we are happy and if we have money, we will become happier. If we are miserable, we are suffering, we have power, we have money but what will we do with our power, our money? It is not going to eradicate our illness, our sufferings. There are people who remain miserable even when they are living in palaces. It does not mean we should renounce things. Nothing will happen either by leaving behind things or by clinging to them.

Happiness depends on us, on our state of consciousness or unconsciousness, whether we are asleep or awake. If we are asleep, then a few sensations of the body like food, sex give happiness to us. We confuse happiness with pleasure of the senses. We live for small thrills. Our life is very superficial; it has no depth, no quality, no substance. We live in the world of quantity (more money, more power, more ego). When we are awake, then happiness acquires a totally different meaning. Happiness is more psychological; less physical. An awakened person enjoys nature, beauty, good music, dance, silences and meditation. This happiness is far higher, far deeper than the joy that we gain from food, or sex, or money, or power.

Happiness has no reason from the outside world. We are responsible for our unhappiness, our sufferings. It is our choice. There is no secret behind it.

The desire for total happiness and for ultimate freedom lies dormant in everyone. It is in the form of a seed that contains a tree within it. In its perfectly developed state, it becomes our nature to be happy, to be free. The fruit does not come from outside; the fruit is created within us. This developed tree will bear fruits of happiness.

Happiness comes from within, not from what others think of us. We will not become happy if the outside world changes, but only if we change. *Gurus* can give us the techniques or may guide us about the path, the way, but that is all the *guru* can do. The rest is up to us.

Happiness is where we are; no matter where we are, happiness is there. It surrounds us. Happiness is not to be sought; it is happiness that the universe is made of and we are missing it because we look sideways. We have to look directly at the present. If we look in the past or future, then we miss it. Don't remain lost in the jungle of pleasures; rise a little higher to reach happiness. We are unable to recognise happiness because we hide behind the walls of money, of power, of ego.

Happiness happens when we are truly awake. In this awakened state, we experience wisdom. When we get *gyana* at an inner, psychological level, we feel peaceful and this peace brings happiness. Fears diminish and disappear as wisdom dissolves fear. Because we are fearless, we need not insulate ourselves from physical, mental and emotional insecurities.

Happiness has no roots in power and fame; it is found only in self-realisation. Ultimate happiness occurs only when we are truly awakened; sleep is gone and dreams are lost. When our whole body feels enlightened, there is no darkness felt within. The ego is gone; all anxiety, anguish, tensions disappear. We are in a state of total contentment. We live in the present, there is no past, no future.

This moment is everything. Suddenly the whole sky drops into us. This is bliss; this is real happiness. To experience bliss is our birthright.

Bliss is without any opposition. It is serene and tranquil. It is ecstasy without excitement. Ecstasy is when we are happy without any reason. All reasons arise from outside. This bliss is proof of our *tyag*, our renunciation. Bliss is the measuring scale. There is no other proof of our detachment, except for bliss. Bliss will prove whether our renunciation is true or false.

There is no point in giving up our home, our money, wearing saffron robes and going to the Himalayas or sitting on the banks of River Ganges, but if we are not happy or blissful, then all these things are worth nothing but are a mere deception. If a *sannyasi* (sage) seems unhappy, it means his *sannyas* is fake; he is unable to control his *indriya*, his senses. That is why he is unable to detach himself from the world and he feels unhappy. Only detachment can make renunciation blissful. Without *tyag*, there is no happiness, no peace. How can there be any bliss without any peace?

Happiness depends on unhappiness. Bliss is transcendence, that is it means moving beyond the state of happiness and unhappiness. Pleasure is dependent on others; happiness is not dependent on others. Bliss is our very being. Pleasure binds us to sex, to food, to comfort. It is bondage; it chains us. Happiness gives us a little bit of freedom. Bliss is absolute freedom; it gives us wings. We feel light. It gives us joy.

The *Gita* differentiates between transient happiness or happiness derived from the senses called *kama* and *raag* and ultimate happiness (*sukha-prasanna-chita*).

Happiness depending on *kama* and *raag* is transient and is soon replaced by discontentment. The *Gita* encourages us to seek permanent happiness.

Krishna says:

*'Don't get dictated by your senses (indriya). Develop the ability to withdraw your senses the way a tortoise withdraws its limbs within.' Once this art is mastered, then a man can walk in this material world, free of likes and dislikes. The mind becomes peaceful. When the mind is at peace, sorrows wither away. Such a man is neither perturbed by sorrow, nor hankers after*

*happiness. He simply is happy or santhusht.*

Krishna explains further:

'Sattvic *or pure happiness is one that arises from spiritual intelligence. In the beginning, it seems like poison (due to intellectual, emotional and physical discipline) but in the end, it is like nectar.'*

'Rajasic *or result-oriented happiness that arises from the senses and sense objects is like nectar in the beginning, but is poison in the end because of its dependency on results and external entities.'* 'Tamasic *or slothful happiness is one that arises from sloth, excessive sleep and irresponsibility and deludes the self from beginning till the end.'* A happiness that results in mental peace is internal and independent of any external source. It comes from renouncing the *karmaphal,* while residing in the material world. Freedom from considering oneself to be the 'doer' of any action is happiness. Doing actions with a sense of detachment is happiness. Once a person is in full control of his physical, emotional and intellectual being to regulate consciousness through silence and meditation, he breaks the cycle of pain and pleasure. Such a person reaches a blissful state.

This is union with the Divine, a *sakshatkar.*

*'To attain this bliss is to attain God.'*

**Happiness**

- Abounding desire is the path to true happiness.
- For want of happiness, create the cause.
- Believing that if we get what we desire is happiness is a big mistake.
- True happiness lies beyond the materialistic world.
- If there is too much happiness, it becomes meaningless.
- It is foolish to believe that happiness lies in temporal, transient things.

Wisdom cannot be found in books. It is not a collection of ideas. As part of the gift of life, we are given a free will and the ability to reason. So, we have the choice to handle the situation according to our wisdom.

Wisdom calls for a totally different way of looking at the reality. It is the only way to explore the hidden potential that any human being possesses. Wisdom helps us to convert our free will at the time of difficulty into a correct and sensible decision. Wisdom removes doubts and confusion in our mind and we ourselves become wisdom, a kind of knowledge. Wisdom is self-development, a choice to consciously grow and evolve. It is a conscious process as it makes us decide consciously each and every time we plan any action.

*Gyana* shows us the meaninglessness of earthly pleasures. When we feel, name, fame, money seem futile and materialism has no meaning for us, it becomes the seed of right understanding that has sprouted in us. Until the material world seems useless to us, we cannot attain right understanding. *Gyana* is the difference between right and wrong. Wisdom is when we become desireless and are contented and happy with whatever we earn and gain through our own labour through honesty and hard work. Wisdom teaches that *maya* is an illusion. Illusion means something which was not yesterday but which is today and will not be there again tomorrow. Be conscious and stay in the present moment. Don't think about the past or future.

Human life should have some meaning and values and without a meaning, we will never be able to lead a rich and dignified life, no matter how much money we have. Richness comes when a life is well lived with purpose and soulfulness, with dignity and grace.

Wisdom is when we understand that the earth is the place to experience both hell and heaven. Actually, heaven and hell are within oneself. Wisdom is heaven and ignorance is hell.

When we are free from attachment to money, we enjoy with whatever money we have and that is heaven, *swarga*. We enjoy heaven on earth. Heaven means we become attachment-free. On the other hand, when we are attached to money, we fear to lose it and are scared to spend it, thinking,that what will happen tomorrow? We live for tomorrow and that tomorrow never comes. We keep on accumulating wealth but are scared to spend; is it not hell? Another hell is begging for anything from others; self-reliance is heaven.

We cannot progress on the path of happiness and peace as we harbour all kinds of dreams. To live life completely, we have to go beyond our needs and live life in freedom. Be magnanimous; be generous. We are finding pleasure in insignificant and not so important things in life, considering it to be happiness. We have to give up greed and miserliness to experience true happiness. *Gyana* shows us the futility of earthly pleasures. The fear of losing, whatever we have, means bondage. If we are not fearless, we cannot have a peaceful mind. For happiness, a peaceful mind is very essential. Happiness comes when we are not scared of losing. Today this body is here, but tomorrow it will perish. Life and world are ever changing. We are unhappy because we have made a home here and are attached to this home. Unhappiness is the result of being attached to things that are transient. If we want to be happy, we should not spend too much time on what is ultimately useless. We view life as we want it to be, It all depends on our own definition.

Wisdom teaches us that we have accumulated the clutters and only we can declutter ourselves. Nobody can help us in our journey. If somebody like a *guru* or a teacher assures any help, it is not possible. We continue to clutter our life by treating life in the wrong way and expecting the *guru* or teacher to help us. Our problem is that we don't know ourselves or our capacity to handle situations. That's why we keep running after *gurus* to seek *gyana.* Whatever valuable is present, is within us; useless things are outside. Trash is outside while true wealth is inside. Hell is outside, heaven is inside. '*Outside is the world; inside is the happiness,*' The day we give up our illusion, we will be surprised to realise that we don't need any outside help. We will realise that we have wasted so much of our time seeking outside help and have missed a lot of happiness in the process. We were miserable without any reason; misery was merely in our mind.

If we want to wake up, then this is the time to wake up. Wake up this very moment. We will notice that there is nothing to be done; only do *nishkam karma.* Doing selfless *karma* means that nothing else needs to be done. Our problems are solved because selfless *karma* takes us to the path of peace and happiness. This path will show us that there never was any problem, or any disease.

We should consider ourself very fortunate that we have got the chance to remove our negative emotions which were hidden inside. Negativity is a serious disease; it has to be thrown out. Once the disease is thrown out, our inner self appears very pure and calm. But, to reach there we have to put in a lot of effort. It is not to be brought from anywhere. The result is hidden in our actions, our deeds.

Spirituality is a search for the meaning in life. Wisdom, especially spiritual wisdom, is not just about 'knowing'; it is about 'applying'. Applying knowledge is true wisdom. Spiritual wisdom is 'knowing' the soul as opposed to material and physical things in the world. When we understand this, the shift in priorities allows us to embrace spirituality in a more profound way. A spiritual person is one whose highest priority is to love oneself and others. Spiritual wisdom is unbiased judgement, self-knowledge, non-attachment, ethics and self-transcendence. A spiritually wise person develops many qualities, such as humility, integrity, compassion, empathy, honesty, justice and innocence. Such qualities are essential and we cannot continue to function for long if we ignore and dismiss these qualities. Those who are atheists, agnostics and sceptics are beyond spiritual understanding. But there are others, who are faithful in their understanding of spiritual life. They are called introspective devotees and *nishkam karmayogi*, because they understand that beyond this material world lies the spiritual world.

There are those who try to understand the Supreme by cultivating knowledge, *gyana*' and they can be counted among Krishna's favourites.

As Krishna says:

*'There is a very intimate relationship between me and all the devotees, but he who is a* gyani, *knowledgeable of me, I consider that* gyani *to be just like my own self. That* gyani *is always in my heart and I am always in the heart of the* gyani. *Pure devotees, full of* gyana, *are never out of spiritual touch, and therefore, they are very dear to me.'*

Only through *gyana* can a person easily neutralise his sinful actions. How is it possible for one engaged in *bhakti*, selfless *karma* and *gyana* to not get purified from sinful activities?

*Gyana* has the power to eliminate all kinds of reactions to sinful deeds.

In the *Gita*, Krishna explains:

*'This material world is a tree, whose roots are upwards and branches are below.'*

(If one stands on the bank of a river, or any reservoir of water, he can see that the trees, reflected in the water, are upside down. The branches go downwards and the roots, upwards).

Krishna says in the *Gita*,

*'There is an imperishable banyan tree* (peepal *tree) having its roots as* Brahman, Paramatma *and whose stem is represented*

*as Brahma, the Creator and whose leaves are the* Vedas. *One who knows the tree is the knower of* the Vedas.' The entanglement of this material world is compared to a banyan tree. The tree of this material world has no end and the one who is attached to this tree, cannot get *gyana,* liberation. The material reflection of the real tree has to be cut off. When a person understands the *Vedas*, when he understands that the ritualistic formula of the *Vedas* is materialism, he becomes wise.

*Gyana* is to cut down this tree, whose branches extend downwards and upwards and nourished by the three modes of material nature. When we cut down this tree, we see the real tree of the spiritual world.

The material world is but a shadow of reality. In the desert, there is no water, but the mirage suggests that there is water. *Gyanayoga* explains that we are associated with the three modes of material nature—*sattva, rajasa* and *tamas.* We must transcend from the three modes of nature to attain peace and joy.

*Bhakti, nishkam karma* and *sankhya (gyana)* help us in *transcendental growth.* This is spiritual wisdom, which means knowing self.

Now you may ask how can we know whether one has attained wisdom?

Krishna says:

*'One who is not disturbed in the mind, even in threefold miseries, or elated when there is happiness, and who is free from attachment, fear and anger, is called a sage with a steady mind.'*

Unless one is able to follow the do's and dont's, it is not possible to attain a steady mind.

Krishna says:

*'One who is able to withdraw his senses from the sense objects, as the tortoise draws its limbs within its shell, is firmly fixed in perfect consciousness.'*

When our mind becomes free of all desires and is innocent

like a child, in that state we become a saint. A true saint is beyond conditions and rules as he lives totally within and not externally.

A saint is one who gives up whatever is transient. It is possible because everything is within us. We are born with all the means inside us, but these means have to be attuned to awaken oneself.

Once we attain inner peace, we are in control of our mind. The higher stages of this process, once we have attained inner peace, grow into *gyana*, which is wisdom. This wisdom makes us tolerant. There are no enemies. Our creative abilities are activated and we become very organised without any effort and the mind gets decluttered. There is no chaos. This is ultimate stage of peace; a tranquil mind. Inner peace and wisdom guide us to a perfect spiritual path. This is self-realisation.

True wisdom is when we experience the self (soul).

Krishna says:

*'There are three gates leading to the hell of self-destruction for the soul—lust, anger and greed. Every sane man should give up, for they lead to the degradation of the soul.'*

They are the root cause of virtually every single problem in human life. A wise man, who does not want to slide down to the lowest, must try to give up these three enemies. So, lust, anger and greed actually disturb the balance of mind and soul. They block the spiritual path and therefore are called the gateway to hell. As soon as lust, anger and greed are abandoned, all other demoniac vices and evils dissolve and dissipate. Hence, one should be extremely vigilant about these three doors and keep far away from them. Lust, greed and anger are the foundations for all other vices and sins.

According to Krishna:

*'Wisdom is humility, pridelessness, non-violence, tolerance, simplicity, cleanliness, steadiness, self-control, renunciation of objects of sense gratification, absence of false ego, detachment,*

*even-mindedness amid pleasant and unpleasant events,* bhakti *and* vairagya, *self-realisation and search for Absolute Truth –all these are considered as knowledge (wisdom) and contrary to it is ignorance.'*

The process of *gyana* is sometimes misunderstood by an unwise being, but actually this is the real process of knowledge. This process is just like a staircase, beginning from the ground floor and going up to the top floor.

*Karma* seeds can be stopped from sowing only through wisdom. Sinful desire seed can be removed only by acquiring wisdom.

Wisdom is a tried and tested way teaching us to go beyond superstitions and against blind faith. People's understanding about the *Vedas* as a ritual is not wisdom. Rituals make us materialistic and we remain stuck in the cycle of birth and death. If we are a materialist, it means we are ignorant. We are not giving a chance to nature, to divine, to enlighten us and fill us with *gyana*. Wisdom is the light within us to convert inner emptiness into a fulfilment. Wisdom is the real wealth, which brings contentment, fearlessness and peace. A fragrance of restfulness begins to emerge from us. At this stage of *gyana,* we reach that point where pleasure and pain, gain and loss, victory and defeat become similar.

Wisdom communicates, while logical intelligence criticises. Logic tells where the difference is, while wisdom shows where unity is. Logic analyses, wisdom combines. By taking the path of *gyana*, man can defeat all his obstacles, all his sufferings. Wisdom alone can make us aware of our bad deeds, wrong actions. The more we apply wisdom, the less we become materially attached. Even the seeds of past *karma* cannot germinate as they get burned in the fire of wisdom.

To criticise *varna* is not wisdom. We need to understand the reason behind it. Wisdom is when we understand that *karma* decides our *varna*. In *Bhagvad Gita*, Krishna points out:

*'Four natural divisions, Brahmin, Kshatriya, Vaishnava and Shudra—in the human society are created by Him. These divisions are not based on birth, but are according to the three modes of material nature (*sattva, rajasa, tamas*) and the work associated with them.'*

We can upgrade ourselves by transcending the *trigunas* and become like Rishi Valmiki.

At the time of death, at the last moment, our mind is full of whatever we have done in our life. We cannot suddenly change ourselves at the time of death. Death is the sum of our whole life. Reading chapter 2, chapter 8 and chapter 18 of Bhagvad *Gita* at the time of death, does not help the dying person,as it is living the *Gita*, not just listening the *Gita* at the moment of death.

'Whatever occupies the mind at the time of death determines the destination of the dying.' One's thoughts and behaviour during the course of one's life accumulate to influence one's thoughts at the moment of death. So, this life creates one's next life. If we live our present life in the mode of goodness, doing selfless *karma* and *bhakti*, then it is possible for one to remember God at the time of death. Then, the next body will be transcendental (spiritual) and not material.

Death is not going to ask you how many scriptures have you read?

At the time of death, only what we have known ourselves will remain with us. What was borrowed by us from others will be lost. A borrowed scripture's knowledge is useless, but if a *Gita* is revealed to us and we are living the *Gita*, in our day-to-day life, then they are expressions of our own realisation. We have attained *gyana*, wisdom, which takes us to the path of enlightenment.

Death is a God-given gift. It is a great opportunity to pass through. If we can die alert, conscious and aware, we will never be born again, which means *moksha*.

Man inherits *knowledge* and it does not come from outside. All knowledge is covered and the process of uncovering is called *learning*. When the veil is removed, there is more '*knowing*'. If the veil is thick, it is ignorance. When the veil is entirely gone, wisdom appears. This veil can be removed automatically if we do detach *karma* and *nishkam bhakti.* Then God destroys the darkness from our heart with the lamp of wisdom. By the light of God's divine power, the darkness of the material energy is dispelled.

We can clean our inner slate and purify ourselves through wisdom. If we honestly regret and repent for our previous actions, we notice inner changes in us. We become detached from *mohamaya* without much effort. We understand the meaning of peace and happiness which cannot be bought by money. Our soul, which was heavily covered with worldly attachments, becomes free and we see the *light* (soul) and this is '*enlightenment*'.

Wisdom helps us to see the *light* and teaches us that the journey is long, and destinations are peace and happiness. Aim at the destination and do not accept anything less than inner happiness.

Find your Light, find your Truth, your Purpose, and live it. The path that is shown by your Light is the only Path and that is the right Path for you.

Our outside is not important; our inside is our existence, the main personality, the essence.

We may look very peaceful externally while we may be very disturbed within. There is no judge. We are the judge and responsible for our own self.

*'It is not possible for the human being to be happy without understanding the* gyanayoga.'

□

# Knowing 'Self' is Knowing God

*'Touch all the three paths (*karma, bhakti, gyana*), so that nothing remains untouched and you get connected to Brahman.'*

# Knowing 'Self' is Knowing God

## Spirituality

Spirituality is a search for the 'self'. We have to know who we are, and once we know who we are, we will attain the truth without leaving the world. The body is sometimes called the vehicle of the soul, according to spiritual literature. Actually, the body is just as spiritual as the soul. Spirituality has nothing to do with renouncing anything. In fact, a spiritual being will be able to enjoy everything more intensely, more totally than the materialist. A materialist's life is very superficial. On the other hand, spirituality is life in depth. We are centred at our very being. We can go on living on the circumference, moving freely anywhere, but still remaining at the centre. If we are at the centre, then there is no problem. We know who we are. Our identity is at the centre. We enjoy food, clothes, we enjoy a beautiful house, we enjoy music, dance. There is no problem, there is no need to renounce life. The modern-time spirituality is different from the old school of spirituality. The message is: Don't renounce but stay at the centre.

There are people who do meditation every day without being conscious of what is right and what is wrong. We can belong to a spiritual group and devotedly follow the teachings of the *satsang*, yet we are judgmental towards others' life. It means we are not spiritual. There are many people who do not practice religion, who do not meditate, pray or belong to any spiritual group, yet they are very spiritual people. These people naturally do things for others. They think on how they can help people in need. Their thoughts are kind, rather than judgmental towards others. We find them kind, loving and caring towards themselves and towards others.

There are many religious people, who are anything but kind. They are religious but extremely judgmental, egoistic and superficial. We can be both religious as well as spiritual, but only when we are doing it from the heart rather than superficially.

For those who wish to climb the mountain of spirituality, the path is love, compassion and selflessness. By taking the spiritual path, man can defeat all his earthly obstacles. The desire to enjoy worldly pleasures kills in us the sense of spirituality.

Spiritual awakening is not a state. We don't have to go to the Himalayas to find it. It cannot be transferred to us by a *guru*, nor can it be taken away or lost. We do not have to become anyone's disciple or follower. Spirituality is about radically opening up to this extraordinary gift of life. Spirituality is not a destination; it is our nature. It is our birthright to discover the magical power hidden within. Man should know the difference between the material and spiritual worlds. If we are looking for spirituality, we have to become our own guide. No *gurus* or masters can help us. Spirituality means knowing the 'self' (soul). So, how can anybody else help us in knowing our own self? If we are putting effort and trying to become our own guide, we notice that God has become our true guide and guru. We give power to God and we gain power. We have to forgo our ego in giving power to God and we notice that we are growing in spirituality and gaining more power. At this stage self-importance becomes the biggest hurdle. In spirituality, self-importance can stop progress for a long time. But once we stop giving importance to ourselves and start trusting God, we feel our struggles in life are becoming less, because self-importance is the biggest block in the path of spirituality. There are many instances where *sannyasis*, who gave self-importance to their spiritual achievements, turned to commercialism and accepted the material platform.

The advanced stage of spirituality can be described as being detached in a peaceful state of deep meditation. Very few worldly people accept it, and those who do, generally stay outside the society. For saints and *sannyasis*, it is possible but for the *sansarik* (worldly), it is difficult though not impossible. It is not easy to know the 'self', but through *nishkam karmayoga* we can know 'self', which means knowing God. Once we are a *karmayogi*, we can know God with God's Grace. *Karmayoga* opens the door to *Gganayoga*, which is ultimate, because this is given to us by God Himself by enlightening our inner world. This inner awakening takes us close to God and heals the fear of death, removes desire, lust and destroys anger. Understanding of the inner self gives the ultimate meaning to life and shows us that God is the only thing that is real. This *gyana* makes the mystery of life effortlessly clear, helping us to enjoy the fulfilment of life's purpose, which is to love God with our whole mind, soul and heart. We learn to love others as we love ourselves. Knowing the inner is true knowing, which washes away all preconceived ideas and dogmatic obstacles from our mind. This can change our life, take us to consciousness and connect us to the divine. This leads us to our marvellous advancement, which is beyond the materialistic world.

Love is knowing God, God can only be known in Love because in love ego disappears. People with great heart or great insight can fathom God. We have to be very clear about our part and God's part. It is a very delicate balancing act. At this stage, we should know what we need to do and what we need to avoid. After attaining spirituality, we get the inner power to face the world. The world does not change; it remains the same. Only we get inner strength. We become detached, we become fearless, we become anger-free, we feel that being born as a human is a blessed state. We are peaceful and happy. People around us don't acknowledge this. They criticise us; they say our *bhakti* is fake, our remembering God all the time is a drama because for them remembering God is only by visiting temples or remembering God during times of crises. They forget that God is not in temples or in the sky. He is surrounding our inner sky. We can search for Him within ourselves, not outside.

It does not matter if we are not successful in the beginning, but we cannot be contented until we have reached there. Being a *sharanagati* (complete surrender) to the divine, is the path for higher knowledge. We trust God and He knows how to provide security to His devotees. The divine order arranges our future more wisely than we ourselves can. When we reach this state, then nobody can take away from us what is divine. However, much we attain God, it can never be snatched by others. And there is no competition, or fear of losing, because if one can attain, the others too can attain. Divine is the only thing which does not become less if one attains it; rather, it becomes available in greater quantity. When Krishna gave *Gita ka gyan*, it was for everybody. Millions attained knowledge. We should not keep knowledge about God to ourself; we should spread it. Everything will remain here; only knowledge will go with us. Acknowledge the truth that God is both existent and knowable. God exists in everything that exists in this world. Acknowledgement of this truth is the purpose of spiritual life. This spirituality takes us on the path of clarity, peace, joy and happiness. At this state of spirituality, we come to know that God is not to be afraid of, but should be loved instead. When we are spiritually awakened, we understand that those He punishes, must be wrong. If something bad happens, I must have committed a sin, even if I am not aware of it. If we are a spiritual being, we will look deep enough until we find the flaw. God is always right otherwise this world would have become a dangerous place to live in.

If we fear God, we will not move to the higher level. God is not to be afraid of, but to be loved. God answers our prayers. God is impartial. God approves work, competition and winning, but in an honest manner. We cannot understand this until spiritual growth has been achieved.

The nature of *samsara* is such that people will worship God because He has tremendous qualities to get attracted to. For all the worldly people, God should be the goal to attain because God represents the most desirable qualities in creation, namely strength, fame, wealth, knowledge, beauty and detachment. We feel safe in God's company. We cannot doubt Him. If we doubt Him, it means that we are doubting 'self'. Belief in God is very, very important. If we believe in a stone, in a rock, we get automatically to believe in God. When we trust God, we start accepting things. We are sure that God supports what is best for us, not just what our imagination dictates. Spirituality makes us aware of this. The spiritual journey takes us to the place where we begin to know the 'self', a point of consciousness.

## Knowing 'Self'

By not knowing who we are, by not knowing what God is, by not knowing how to connect with the soul, a materialist falls into sin. Spirituality is not accepted by the materialistic world. Therefore they are devoid of peace and happiness. No human being is perfect. Everyone makes some mistake. But after knowing 'self', a *gyani* adapts to things easily, while a materialist stays stubborn because he thinks he is in charge of how things should work, how things should happen. If we go on holding on to life, then we deprive ourselves of freedom of life. We must just detach ourselves from materialism and see how God showers self-realisation on us. God distributes happiness and we get it every day. We are not worried about tomorrow; rather we will be thankful to God for giving us more than we deserve. We will notice that God gave when we were not expecting it at all. Our life journey becomes very smooth, we become detached and engaged at the same time. If we want to attain all this, *spiritual power* is necessary.

Faith in God and being spiritual constitute the way to open the lines of communication. The spiritual path makes us understand how the inner world can be more thrilling than anything outside. The emptiness of outward life becomes irrelevant. We become comfortable to live with ourself. We learn to tackle difficult situations, difficult people with ease and comfort. We begin to understand how reality works and the human nature starts to unfold its secrets. The inner peace keeps unfolding new stages of the soul. Our calmness and peace become very useful to handle outside problems.

We may be a householder, our inside world is private, but our outer existence has to go on. When we lead a normal life, a very ordinary existence with an extraordinary intensity, with passion, with consciousness, we move on the path of spirituality.

When a person forgets that he has a soul or he is soul and his source is rooted in the Eternal Being, he lives in illusionment. He thinks that only material existence is real and thus becomes totally ignorant of the source which is virtual. When this happens, contact with the source is lost. He cannot hear the voice of the *atma*, as the soul is silent. For a time, this strategy seems to work, but no one can gain complete control over nature. *Prakriti* is at work. The soul has its own project in mind.

These projects described in the *Vedas,* are the five kleshas, or causes of human suffering. They are:

1. Ignorance (*avidya*)
2. Ego (*ahankar*)
3. Attachments (*raga*)
4. Aversion (*dvesha* )
5. Fear of death (*abhinidvesha*) or clinging to life.

How advance and hi-tech the world has become but the five *kleshas* are still relevant. Each *klesha* has its own effect. The strong addiction of money, power ego of every type is well known by all. Man becomes desperate to cling to something and the mind creates an entity, known as ego. As ego has many needs, it begins to fulfil all these needs. This ego is unable to solve the original problem, that is, the ignorance. Trapped in the whirlwind of anger, greed, attachment, egoism, ambition, all the other distractions become the source of suffering. It means that the influence of the soul is crucial. Each *klesha* is at work. Separation from the soul results in pain and suffering. But if we want to get rid of pains and sufferings in our life, the soul provides the solution for the five *kleshas.*

**Ignorance** *(avidya)* is solved by right knowledge as it delves deeper than the material level to find its roots.

***Ego*** *(ahankaar)* when awareness comes, ego takes a back seat.

**Attachment** *(raga)* when wisdom comes, attachment turns into non-attachment.

**Aversion** *(dvesha) is a* strong dislike or hatred. Practicing kindness, love and avoiding discriminatory behaviour can remove *dvesha.*

**Fear of Death** *(Abhinidvesha)* is solved when the soul is experienced directly, since the soul is never born and never dies.

At the last moment, that is, at the time of death, we think of what we have done in our whole life. We cannot suddenly change ourselves at the time of death. Death is summing up of our whole life. If we have been restless all our life, then we will be restless at death also. If we have been peaceful throughout, then our death will be very peaceful.

Krishna says:

*'Whatever state of being one remembers when he quits his body, that state he will attain without fail.'*

If in our present life, we live in the mode of goodness and always think of God, it is possible for us to remember God at the end of our life. If the whole of our life, we have been attached to materialism, then we will be attached to money when dying too. At the moment of death, the whole of life shrinks and comes near, with the essence of life appearing in front of us. We cannot become a *religious person* at the end of our life. If we wake up today, then gradually we will be able to take care in the future.

At the time of death, by reciting the *mantras* or by reading the *Gita* near us will not purify our soul, because at that time, we will not be able to hear it. We were attached to materialism throughout our life, and at the time of death also we will remain a materialist.

Good deeds and *bhakti* are the arts to make death a grandeur.

We are complete and happy when *gyana, bhakti* and *karma* are properly adjusted and attuned. Everything is within us. We need to awaken our dormant power to adjust and attune. We are born with all the means and need not go to logics to awaken ourself. Do not doubt the inner strength.

We see life as we want to see it. It all depends on our own definitions. We build up a world of our own beliefs and we go on living in it. Keeping those beliefs, we go on finding our own reasons. This is the root cause of our suffering because we are ignorant about our real identity. We are ignorant so we keep on accumulating *karmic* seeds by attaching ourselves to *senses*. These seeds do not manifest (*aprarabdha*) in the beginning, but if we keep on collecting these seeds, they manifest as suffering, which becomes *prarabdha*, not only in this life but even in the next births.

God has made the human being so that he should rise up as master of *maya*. *Maya* is the magical power of illusion that underlies the phenomenal world. The sole function of *maya* is to attempt to divert man from the *atma* (soul) to *sansara* (world), from reality to unreality. *Maya* is the base and it is from the beginning of its structural inherence in the phenomenal world. Man's forgetfulness of his soul is the root cause of all other forms of suffering. Inner reforms lead to outer reforms. After inner reforms, we will find that outward reform is always possible. The human mind, full of clutter, leads a repulsive life of a world of delusion (*maya*). All these illusions are inner enemies. They are not physically existent but which can be overcome by our power, our might.

For knowing self, there is no need to follow complicated methods. Selfless love for God makes Him appear in front of us. Knowing means transformation. Transformation can only happen when we change the movement and the direction of our consciousness. Through wisdom one can attain the highest spiritual consciousness. For knowing 'self' we need a lot of energy. Saving energy ensures energy accumulation that allows us to be more conscious and aware. *Patanjali yogasutras* are the observances that aim to prevent energy from seeping out.

One of the biggest sources of energy depletion is negative emotion. Overcoming negative emotion is a big part of spiritual practice. Silence should be maintained as too much talk can leak the energy pool. When we are alone, we daydream a lot. An act of imagination can become an activity, which is a significant part of energy leakage. Observing oneself and watching the moment is important to transfer energy to our energy pool. Knowing 'self' depends on the level of inner purity that helps us to start noticing the insights through conscious effort. It allows us to access finer impressions. It means our consciousness should not flicker; it should be stable.

Knowing 'self' is awakening of the right understanding. When we know the difference between right and wrong, it becomes 'knowing self'. We feel a transformation inside us. This is blossoming of our consciousness, the opening of lotus inside us. At this stage, we touch that space where there is no mind; something flowers within. We feel awakened! After this awakening, we know our 'self'. We understand the true meaning, which is that '*as a single sun illuminates the whole world, the same way one* atma *illuminates everybody.*' When we are awake, it is spiritual achievement; not an illusion. Without knowing self, every experience is an illusion. The only clear path to God is the path of constant self-awareness.

## Knowing God

*Bhagwan* is the right word to denote God. To consider God as oneself is *knowledge*; to look upon both as different and separate *is duality*, ignorance, *avidya*. We all have the mark of God in us in the form of the eternal soul or *atma*. He who resides in nature is *Bhagwan* (God). We cannot experience closeness to God, near-death experiences, out of body experiences which do not obey the ordinary physical laws. This is a secret and not meant for open discussion. His secret code is an art that man cannot communicate with man; here God alone is the teacher. No sacred book can help us any more. At this stage we must allow God to take over because nothing in the material world stands outside God. We see the natural order of creation, the *prakriti* everywhere. There is tremendous beauty in the simplest of things. The deeper we look, the more astounding this *prakriti* (nature) appears. That is God. If we are not able to notice this nature, it means we are truly not looking. If we try to see nature without doubt, evidence of God would be revealed instantly. We will be able to hear the voice of God, who is omnipotent and omnipresent. God is all over the place. We are God, the trees are God, the birds are God, the Sun, the moon, the God is all over the place. We close our eyes and we think about it, but there is no need to think with our eyes closed. *Live it.* Only by living, we come to know about God. The definition of God is that which was always, which is always and which will be always. Now, the question is if God has presence in everything, that is, He can be experienced. He can be known. It is very important to understand that He is not an object that we can hold and measure. God involves a constant process. To reach to God, we have to go in stages (as explained earlier). The unfolding of God is a process made possible by the brain's ability to unfold its own potential. The brain has the capacity to see spirituality, which is the way to reach God. This spiritual access is in our hands. To know God is the ultimate promise of spirituality and we must consciously participate in this journey. To know God, we have to awaken the dormant brain. A fully awakened brain is the secret of knowing God. It is no wonder that knowing God is called 'awakening'. With meditation (*dhyana*) we can increase our capacity to reach the goal, where the pure being allows us to reveal the infinite creation of God. We have reached the place, which is both the beginning and end of the process of *'knowing*

*God'*. In this process, our inquisitiveness about the soul, God, unfolds in a completely new way. Here truth can replace our doubts. We have reached a point where nobody can shake us from our trust of God. Now we have found a reachable place which is beyond the material world. If someone questions us if there is really a God, we should know who is asking. Is it an atheist, a materialist, or a sufferer? They will not trust us. For others it is a lie, for us it's the truth. An atheist would like us to show God to him, but knowing God is our experience; not an object. We cannot show our experience in physicality. That is our own personal experience of God-realisation.

Our brain, our intelligence is rightly guided only after the mind has acknowledged that we cannot escape the 'spiritual law'. Nothing can be the cause of our downfall; the cause is our own self-control. We should not allow ourselves to become the slaves of materialism. By freeing ourselves from materialism, honestly and mindfully, we open ourselves to the possibility of life without limits.

Knowing God would be impossible if God didn't want Him to be known. We need to seek God's help to attain God. We cannot attain Him with our efforts alone. *'God exists beyond the five senses and human being's existence is because of the five senses.'* So, we can attain God only with the grace of the divine. The day we start asking for the support, we notice that we have that in us. *Bhakti* helps us to know God: if our heart remembers divine at every stage of our life and if we do *bhakti* with a pure heart. A being who attunes himself to Him with deep and intense *bhakti* and meditation, he gets in touch with divine consciousness. God is sending us messages or clues into the physical world. A conscious person will receive them while a materialist will ignore them. If we are attuned to the soul, we notice that a subtle guidance is at work. The deeper attuned a human being is the more he influences the surroundings through his subtle spiritual vibrations. When all the layers of *kama, vasna, anger, mohmaya* are removed, God is revealed. *Paramatma* is one God who is hidden in all the beings, watching over everyone, witnessing everyone and everything.

The ambition of achieving God in this world is very strong, but we don't need to try hard to achieve God. We just need to follow the simple process. Try to understand the five *kleshas.* If after trying hard we are unsuccessful, it means our attraction to the material world still exists. It is very important to know that knowing God involves a constant process. To reach God, we have to go by stages. We have to outline the entire spiritual journey through *nishkam karma, bhakti* and *gyana.* To know God, we must consciously participate in the journey of free will. To know God, we have to awaken the dormant brain.

God does not require us; we require God. The foundation of spirituality requires the recognition of our divinity, the real nature of our souls and the true purpose of existence in the physical form. *Paramatma, Brahman,* God is a loving energy. We are all composed of God. Without God, there is nothing. God is everything. The ability to hear through our ears is *Brahman,* the power to see from our eyes is *Brahman,* the power to smell through our nose is *Brahman,* though God is unseen, unknowable and yet contains the potential of everything.

*'God is* Paramatma*, the soul, and we beings are the* jeevaatma*, part of* Paramatma*. So, we all are one. The soul has no race, no religion.'*

God and religion have been misunderstood, distorted from centuries and consciously manipulated by mankind. But for God, there is no discrimination. God causes the same Sun to shine on us all, the same rain for everyone. God's name, perhaps, is the ultimate symbol of peace, love, and compassion. God is peace. God is love. Someone who has experienced God surely looks on the entire world with happiness and joy. God-believers are happier, wiser and more successful than the non-believers.

God and our soul are in perfect communication, but to understand this we need *gyana.* If we are surrounded by *avidya* (ignorance), it will defeat our best intentions. To accept one's own ignorance is the first step towards knowing 'self'. Materialist people don't try to know 'self'. This is because we see what we have within. If we don't see God, it is because we see what we have within. If we don't think of God, how can we see God? The one who indulges in worldly pleasures all the time is not in touch with the divine.

According to the *Vedanta*:

*'An ignorant man engrossed in duality desires material things. The intelligent man (seeker) desires enlightenment; but the wise man who understands Oneness just loves and receives everything.'*

## Duality

*'Duality'* means two. When the mind has two paths, two ways, two alternatives for everything, it's been called *duality* of mind. When we are divided into two—negative/positive, darkness/light, man/ woman, energy goes downward. Duality is a mind's creation, created by a clinging and attached mind. Where there is 'I', it creates duality. If we go outwards, we will move into the world of duality. Duality is the experience of life, where one chooses to judge people, places and things. Duality is living with ego-consciousness. Duality is *'dwaita'.* The mind cannot exist without duality and cannot go beyond two paths, no matter what the situations is.

To rise above the duality of mind, it is important to understand something that is constant, that does not change with the nature of mind; even if the mind changes, it does not change. When we realise something within us that is ever constant, we can rise above the duality of mind. We have to find the constant within us, so that whatever situation arises for us to take a decision, we don't reach to the dual space of mind, but reach the spot within—the '*constant*'. '*When we reach the constant state after self realisation,* we experience every situation of our life for the first time and don't simply act on the situation, but see the past, present, and future of the situation and then make our choice and decision in the moment. Once we have made a choice, our mind remains steady in the moment. If we face any obstacles in the path, we focus on the solution and keep moving on the path.

It is easier to stick to a single path after self-realisation as our only desire remains to become *one* with God. Life is possible beyond the duality of mind. To attain *Brahman*, we have to move from duality to non-duality.

## Non-duality

*Non-duality*: When there is no 'I', then there is non-duality. If we go inwards, we'll move into the world of non-duality. The path is created inward, where we can move beyond the state of confusion and find a place within us which is constant. Non-duality is a state where all the dualities of the mind end. The positive and negative thoughts converge into one. Our mind can produce many paths out of a single situation, but if we are connected within, we figure out the one path and walk on it till the end. When we drop the process of the mind and realise the 'self', we rise above the mind and that is non-duality. We understand the process of life both within us and outside ourselves.

Awareness cannot exist with duality. Enlightenment is the realisation of non-dual. Enlightenment makes us non-dual. When we are already in the transcendental state, we remain undivided and this is *adwaita,* non-duality. Non-duality is a mature state of consciousness in which through 'transcendence' and 'awareness', ONENESS is attained. Although this awareness may seem spontaneous, it usually follows prolonged preparation through practicing *bhakti,* selfless *karma* and meditation. Non-duality is ascribed in *Adwaita Vedanta* as *turiya, sahaja.* The unity of an individual soul called *atman* and supreme soul called *Brahman* is a non-dual state of consciousness. The experience of God (soul) connects us with ONE. With ONENESS, the energy and mind become stable. When we relate ourselves with God, everything that we experience with Him becomes our nature.

When we direct our attention on one, i.e. the constant, be it God or *atma*, slowly our mind begins to pick impressions and experiences of it and we develop more stability inside by being ONE. All the chaos within the mind happens when too much thinking goes on in the mind. When we direct our attention on God, our mind does not have to think much. Rather we keep our mind engaged with ONE.

When we are undivided, non-dual, we transcend. So, the whole effort should be to become undivided, to become ONE. For this, one has to move from duality to non-duality, *dwaita* to *adwaita*. Whatever we see through our mind becomes two. The moment the mind disappears, 'I' also disappears and *once 'I' disappears, we are enlightened*. So, underneath duality, where there is no mind, we will find ONE who can be called God or *nirvana*. We are one with God. Choice is mind, which is dual (two). *When we don't choose*, we experience enlightenment.

Awareness is non-duality, enlightenment. As soon as we are enlightened, 'two' disappears. We take life as death and death again turns into life. Every day turns into night and night turns into day every morning again. So, they are not two; they are one whole. This is non-duality, *adwaita*. This is the most essential part to understand non-duality. This awareness occurs when we transcend. When we have transcended, then duality does not divide us. We remain undivided—*adwaita.*

*'This is what the* Upanishads *teach: be non-dual, be one. To be one means not to choose, because once we choose, our choice divides, which is duality.'*

Krishna says:

*'When the oneness with God is achieved, the distinctions of the various paths disappear.'* Krishna also says;

'Sambhav *means* samanta ka bhav. *When there is* sambhav, *divine is always near.'*

According to Krishna, *sambhav* is when we don't see duality and start seeing the ONE in a friend and in a foe, in good and bad, in sin and virtue, in heaven and hell. Then we start becoming one. If we want to attain ONENESS, then all should be equal to us. Then we are 'united'.

If we want to go beyond duality, we will have to do *sadhana,* spiritual practice. It is difficult to go beyond duality. How will we see the same as ONE, who has harmed us? But with practice of meditation and *sadhana*, that feeling disappears. We experience deep peace. We are not the same as we were yesterday. We have attained *sambhava*. When there is *sambhava,* divine is always with us.

Oneness is union of *atma* and *Paramatma*. *Paramatma* is present in all bodies without distinction. A 'self-knowing' person does not make any distinction because he understands that *Paramatma* is present in everyone's heart. A transcendentalist does not give importance to difference of bodies. He treats every living being with equanimity. Equanimity is a sign of self-realisation. Those who are beyond dualities (*dwaita*) that arise from doubts, achieve liberation, in spite of living in the material world. So we should not waste our energy in the duality of *paap* and *punya*, enemy or friend, life and death, day and night, good or bad. This is the most essential part to understand ONENESS.

When the 'self', the soul is in communion with the higher soul (*Paramatma*), nature automatically obeys the will of the being. This effortless control over nature is described as 'miracles' by those uncomprehending people who are materialist and follow duality.

*'Oneness, union with God, can be achieved by a householder, a* karmayogi.' There is no need to be an ascetic and live in the Himalayas. For a *karmayogi* it is possible through self-effort, *bhakti* and meditation in the privacy of his home to achieve a divine union. There is no need to be dependent on 'theological' beliefs. Yoga and meditation possess a power by which we can prevent any specific thought from arising in our mind. The more and more we be with God, we don't pick things from the past but allow the things to come to the surface. All situations, events and experiences of life become 'God-willing' and we rise above the duality of mind. By making our mind 'one with God', we allow the situation to come to us and we give our best to it. We focus on things that come our way. When we are satisfied within, our role is to serve the *present moment* or present situation and not be worried about the past or the future.

## Silence

God always speaks in silence, so, in our spiritual journey, we should be sensitive and alert about tiny clues. Knowing 'self' is attained in silence; it has nothing to do with words. *Silence means knowing God.*

When we become inwardly so strong, then we are free from attachments. Non-attachments need strength and strong will power. After this, we no longer chase and run after materialism. Our inner world helps us to solve all the difficult situations. We don't need outside help because we rely entirely on the inner world.

When all desires fall, then the inner silence comes naturally. Silence is the only secret to know God. If we want to become quiet within, maintain silence. How much of *puja-path, jaap, mantra* we may do, but if we are unable to control our desires, it will not help in achieving inner silence. When we are decluttered from within, we feel free and empty inside. When we are 'one' with ourselves, we don't want to collect anything because our wealth lies within us. Silence is a totally different phenomenon. It is very positive. Noiselessness is not silence. Silence is a reality which is present in everyone. It is not fictitious; it is a reality. All our senses are external, as they are meant to explore the outside world, but when we turn the same senses inward with the help of silence in meditation, we connect with the inner world and we can see '*light*'. This light we can see only through silence. We connect with the inner world. Our inner world is so beautiful that it has its own fragrance, its own light. No word can describe this, but we can reach there. Meditation and silence open the doors of our inner world. We must just sit, doing nothing and start communicating through silence. Sitting down with peace within means knowing God. God can be attained through silence. Be peaceful within through silence and know God, who knows all.

## Bliss

When we go beyond happiness and misery, that is '*bliss*'. When we are beyond duality, that is '*bliss*'. When there is ONENESS, it is non-duality, a*dwaita.*

ONENESS is the ultimate bliss. By achieving bliss, everything is achieved. There is no greater bliss than this, rest all is misery. '*Bliss is the abode of Brahman.*'

We have no worries, no thoughts, but our heart is full of joy, that is, bliss, which is ecstasy. Bliss and ecstasy are when we are happy without any reason. It is a *unique coincidence*, but it happens.

It happens when we go beyond *karma*, beyond action. When the mind, body and soul are perfectly aligned, when we have the capacity to go beyond the mind and the moment the limitations disappear, bliss arises. Bliss is freedom from all limitations. Bliss cannot be attained with the *mind*. When we start overflowing with energy, it is a delight, it is bliss. We are alone but very happy. When we attain knowledge, devotion exists. Thoughts appear but emotions do not. We have no thoughts, but the heart is full of joy because our inner world is completely balanced.

It is absolutely peaceful because we have transcended from duality. Bliss is more like peace than like happiness. Bliss, in the ancient Indian scripture *Veda,* is *ananda,* one of the three important aspects of creation. *Sat chit ananda* is translated from the *Sanskrit* as 'eternal bliss consciousness', which is the foundation of existence. There are many terms for this, such as enlightenment, *nirvana, moksha.* To experience bliss is a sign of complete enlightenment.

There is no need to go anywhere. We can just sit quietly and do our prayers, our meditation at home. Prayer itself is a joy. Meditation itself is bliss,so why look for it anywhere when it is inside us. If we understand this, then everything happens in that very moment. God Himself showers bliss on us. When we detach ourselves from *mohmaya,* only then can we experience bliss. This bliss is the proof of our renunciation while leading *grihastha jeevan*. For a *karmayogi,* Bliss is the measuring rod of his or her detachment. We are truly detached, means we are blissful.

## God is Light

When we undertake a journey to reach the light, we cannot see the light or achieve the divine straightaway. We should not get disheartened. We have taken the first step to the path. Our soul is covered by attachments, so it has to be uncovered to see the light. Continuous efforts are necessary. A clean-hearted person will achieve this very quickly, while a complicated person may have to work hard to reach there.

Man is afraid of getting rid of knowledge because he fears that he will become ignorant again. But if he clings to this knowledge, he cannot go beyond either. One rises in knowledge by throwing ignorance and one rises into enlightenment by getting rid of knowledge. We are not a light; our whole being is dark. We can know about light, but the knowledge about light will never become light, as long as we have not yet come into contact with the 'inner self'. We have to depend on outside help—scriptures, holy books, etc. but meditation is a very powerful tool to know the inner self. This can help to lead us on the path of enlightenment. There is a deep understanding that one gets on being enlightened, or self-realised. At this state, understanding is not the same as we get through scriptures or holy books. Man realises that there is no duality and understands that the sense of being *separated from existence* is an illusion. This understanding comes from one's experience of reality.

If we are enlightened, it is because we have experienced enlightenment. If someone asks us to prove our enlightenment, we cannot show it to somebody, because it is not an object; it is our experience. Our self-realisation, our experience of enlightenment is above all scriptures. Enlightenment is a non-ending process. It is the beginning, not the end.

*Brahman,Paramatma*, God has presence in the form of light. We can see or feel this light once we attain enlightenment.

As we start going inwards and more inwards, light is seen very clearly. This enlightenment gives *gyana* to understand what is right and what is not right. We start seeing the world as it is. We start accepting people as they are. They don't bother us now, because we are not bothered about the outer world. We do *sakshatkar.*

When all desires disappear, only then God is attained. If we desire to do *sakshatkar*, or want to attain God, we will not be able to succeed because that desire will become an obstacle. When all desires disappear without any condition, when the mind is completely free of desires, it is then that God appears. If our prayers, our meditation are to get something in return, then we will get nothing. *Sakshatkar* is the result of the disappearance of desires. To meet God, we have to become like God. God's *karma* to run this universe is selfless. He showers everything on earth without desiring any return. The moment a person understands that desire cannot be fulfilled and stops desiring, he finds that the divine he was looking for is within him. The desire made him blind to God.

To do *sakshatkar*, we need to go through a process of self-realisation. Self-knowing is not something which we can get all of a sudden. It just goes on advancing. Self-realisation is not an object, but a process. We cannot grab it. If we want to attain spiritualism, we can choose either *bhakti or karmayoga or ganayoga,* the three paths Lord Krishna explained in *Bhagvad Gita*. But we can do the *sakshatkar only* by following all the three paths—*karma*, *bhakti* and *gyana*.

## *Sakshatkar*

We should increase our knowledge to the extent where it helps us to perform detached *karma* and let our *bhakti* be so deep that it reaches the point where it becomes knowledge, *gyana*. When we touch all the three paths so that nothing remains untouched, we get connected to *Parabrahman*. This is the only way to do *sakshatkar*. This path takes us to a different level. We feel grace inside us. Nature starts speaking to us in our language. Miracles start happening around us. Our *sakshatkar* becomes a daily routine. The more we see the divine, the vaster it becomes. *Yeh ek attah sagar hai.* This is an endless ocean. You keep going deep into this sea.

How can we know a person, who has done *sakshatkar* with Brahman?

The answer is that if our heart remembers the divine at every stage of our life, if we do bhakti with a clean heart, without expecting anything in return, the one who is real and who is same both within and outside, whose conscience is not dead, who is awakened from inside and outside, whose every breath is full of truthfulness, whose presence reminds of the divine, if we go near that person whose positive vibration affects us and we feel deep contentment, then that is the proof of that person being engrossed in Brahman. That person has embraced the divine and that being has done *sakshatkar* with Brahman. Only that person can lead us to the right path.

We cannot know Brahman by reading the scriptures; we can know Brahman through experience. On the path of knowing Brahman, we need inner strength and inner depth. Om, Brahman, whose expression in the individual man is *atma* (soul) is *nirguna,* without form or shape. Whether in a human being or a tree root, Brahman means *expansion*. This is a Vedic concept of the divine power of spontaneous growth. The whole essence of *Vedas* is to know *the root,* because Brahman is the root. The conscious fusion of *atma* with Brahman is knowing the *Vedas.*

To understand this, we need to free ourselves from ego, attachments, pretensions, *mohamaya*. *Nishkam karma, bhakti* and *gyana* are the essential and real paths of knowing Brahman.

When *gyana, bhakti* and *karma* meet, there is enlightenment, there is *nirvana*. A combination of the three take us from 'form' (*sakar*) to 'formless' (*nirakar*). When one transcends all dualities and divisions, when one realises the integrity and oneness of life, then it means knowing Brahman, because this state of equanimity and evenness itself is Brahman.

Brahman can be known through awakening, through awareness. Awareness does not change our life, but we begin to see life differently. Inner realisation is awakening. Awareness means knowing self, knowing God—Brahman.

What is awareness?

## Awareness

The ability to understand mysteries beyond human comprehension is awareness. Awareness or ability 'to sense' can be described as one that occurs when the brain is activated in certain ways. Awareness is associated with consciousness, such as a feeling or intuition that accompanies the experience of a phenomenon. It is the state of being conscious of self and one's surroundings. When we are aware, we are fully alive and in harmony with life in this present moment and every moment that follows.

Awareness in the spiritual sense is hard to describe by the intellect. Experiencing awareness is more important than trying to understand it on an intellectual level as it is the most inner part of a being.

Humans have the ability to develop their consciousness (awareness) to an almost unlimited extent, up to the point of knowing the Absolute Truth, the Brahman. Other species do not have this special ability. That is why Vedic scriptures consider human life especially sacred. God's realisation is possible through awakening, consciousness because the real identity of a living being is the soul (*atma*), not the material body. Therefore, man has the chance to gain awareness by raising himself to the highest level of awakening.

If we try to get it by reading scriptures or listening to a discourse or by following a *guru*, we will not be able to know 'awakening' but when it dawns upon us on its own, it will be a life-changing experience. Until then we will think that the mind is a concept which we know but cannot exactly say what it is.

Awareness can be unveiled in everyday living through a slight shift in perception, or paying more attention to our body, mind and soul. There are three steps of awareness and the steps are—be watchful, be alert, aware and conscious, don't go on doing things like a zombie or be a sleepwalker.

We must become aware of our body; be watchful and be alert. When we become aware of our body and its actions, we realise that talking is an art. We find our body is graceful and beautiful. Sometimes if people have difficulties with body awareness, they may appear clumsy, uncoordinated. It is mindfulness of the body which enables us to attain right vision and knowledge. Our body needs constant awareness for the perfect alignment of body and mind. Developing self-awareness by paying attention to the body is the key to making positive changes within ourselves.

When we become aware of our body, then we move deeper into our mind and its activity through imagination. The conscious mind consists of everything within awareness. Awareness of mind is the ability of a person to understand the feelings that are different from his own. When we become aware of the mind, we notice that the mind is occupied with fewer thoughts. If our mind is full of thoughts, it means there is no awareness. As we become more aware there is no energy available for thoughts, they die. When we are hundred per cent thoughtless, the mind becomes absolutely silent. That is the time to move still deeper.

When we bring awareness to the heart by paying attention in a particular way, on purpose, in the present moment, and with a heart that is fully loving unconditionally, we notice that all that is good happens and bad starts disappearing. Love grows and hate disappears; compassion grows and anger disappears, sharing and caring grows and greed disappears. Exactly this is the state when awareness of heart is complete. This awareness is not only good for our emotional heart, but is awfully good for our physical heart as well. We suddenly find ourselves in our being, at the very centre. It is like waking up from a dream and becoming aware of our true identity. When we are awakened, we start separating ourselves from our mind, our body and its physical attributes. Rather we start being more attentive and mindful of what is unfolding now. Without putting any effort, we realise that the cause of suffering is desire and there is a path that leads to the end of suffering. It means 'Awakening' has started its effect on us.

'Waking up' means 'awakening'. Awakening means that'dreaming' is over. Now, we want to know what will happen after awakening? The answer is something which cannot be described! This is beyond the language which we understand. This is an experience beyond words. It is like a dumb man who cannot describe the taste of sugar but can enjoy it. It just cannot be described. We can only experience it. We wake up and see how beautiful the experience is and will repent for not having woken up earlier.

In the deeper state of self-realisation, when our mind is at rest, we will realise chat the mind is an entity in itself. It is a completely noiseless experience which arises from the silence of our mind. This state of awareness, a state of presence, turns into '*knowing*'. This knowing does not require understanding or reasoning. We realise our own truth, our own being. We become detached from outcomes and expectations. We are at peace within and with everything around us.

But for that, we have to spend a lot of time and effort to stabilise our mind. Awakening is not impossible; it is achievable through dedicated practice.

Reaching the state of self-awareness is important and is a state of being conscious and aware of one's body, mind and soul.

The deeper awareness of inner self comes later, after a long spiritual and self-purification by following *sattvic* practices. Meditation is an important yoga practice and one of the most powerful tools to help one find the inner self, to calm and silence the mind and to attain self-awareness.

Awareness, consciousness, awakening is the life force within. It is the depth of our being, understanding the Creator and the Eternal. This is the ultimate purity!

This is enlightenment!

Awakening is the inner experience that leads to *moksha*, liberation.

## Brahman

Brahman is the ultimate reality in the universe. It is formless, genderless, infinite, eternal truth and bliss. It does not change, yet is the cause of all changes. Brahman is the single binding unity behind diversity, in all that exists in the universe. Brahman is a Vedic-Sanskrit word and is a key concept found in the *Vedas*. Brahman is essentially discussed in the *Upanishads* and is described as *sat-chit-ananda* (truth-consciousness-bliss) and as the unchanging, permanent, highest reality. In *Advaita Vedanta*, Brahman is identical to *atma*, is present everywhere and inside each living being and there is *connected spiritual oneness* in all existence.

It is not easy to understand Brahman because, 'the Ultimate is not only the unknown; the Brahman is not only the *unknown*; it is knowable also. We can know it, but we cannot know it totally, because we are just a part of it and the part cannot know the whole. But also, the part cannot be totally ignored either because it belongs to the whole; it is a part of the whole. So, it is understandable in a way, but it cannot comprehend the total because the total is so vast.' The first sound or vibration emerging from the silence is 'Om'. When we chant 'Om', it draws our awareness back to the dawn of creation and into oneness. 'Om' represents the unmanifest and absolute existence. Brahman or the absolute are all synonymous terms pointing to one being. 'Om' is the eternal sound, *pranava*. 'Om' is the sound, the alliance between nature and man, *purush* and *prakriti*.. With 'Om' chant, man can obtain control over all natural manifestations. A man can possess remarkable powers by chanting 'Om'.

In the Vedic hymns, the word 'OM' is always found. Vibrations of 'OM' chanting help in advancement of 'Knowing self'. One cannot achieve transcendental knowledge without understanding Brahman and Brahman is 'Om'.

'OM', the Bliss, is heard in meditation and reveals to devotees the ultimate Truth, the Brahman.

We start enjoying solitude, *vairagya*. The emptiness of outside life becomes irrelevant. The inner peace keeps unfolding new stages of the soul. We become comfortable to live with ourself.

So be in silence. The Lord is heard only in the immaculate silences. The devotee, who is attuned and in silence, the 'Om' vibrations, the primal sound, instantly translate themselves into bliss, the Absolute Identity. In the *Vedanta*, the only real thing is eternal bliss, *sat-chit-ananda*. The timeless waits when the temporary expires; bliss outlives pleasure.

A journey begins in mystery and silence ends with knowing 'self', that is, it means 'knowing God'. If we go on holding on to life, then we are depriving ourselves of *amrit*, the nectar. We will only see death. The moment we become detached, we accept death within and we start seeing the life within. Nectar and death are hidden within us.

*'Soul is the ultimate entity of our being. It has no beginning, no end. It is everywhere, from atoms to endless vast universe. It was there, when there was nothing, it will be there when everything ends. If you understand this, you know 'soul' you know Brahman.'*

Knowing Brahman is ecstasy. Ecstasy means blossoming of the flower. Until the flowers of our inner world do not blossom, we will remain unhappy. Total dependence on God as the sole life comes from our recognition of total bliss, ecstasy. Be attuned with Him and experience boundless joy. When we experience Brahman, all dualities disappear. It is total bliss. We cannot define it. We cannot describe it. We can only experience it. 'Brahman *means* ananda *through divine union.'*

**Union with Self is knowing *Brahman***

*Vedanta* explains: '*No sacred texts can help you any more. No* gurus, *no teachers; only awareness.' Upanishads* say that human consciousness has four states.

One: While you are awake, the waking consciousness. Second: While you are dreaming, the dreaming consciousness.

Third: While you are fast asleep and there is no dream, the sleeping consciousness.

And beyond these threes is the fourth which is *turiya*. *Turiya* means total awareness. The fourth is the state where we realise Brahman. This is the Ultimate Reality. That which cannot be cancelled by anything is the final, the Ultimate, the Absolute Truth.

When we reach this state, all experiences of kundalini arise in us, opening the *chākras,* the lotus, showering the light start disappearing because they are all experiences. Enlightenment is when there is no experience and we are alone. There is nothing to experience; only witnessing, *silently witnessing nothing—shunaya.* Then we have arrived. This is *samadhi.* Witnessing nothing is *samadhi,* nothingness, emptiness, *nirvana.* Enlightenment is when the light is there and it falls on nothing.

*'Experiences mean the 'world'; no experience means 'liberation.'*

## Samadhi

*'You are one with God is samadhi.' Samadhi* means solution. *Samadhi* is when we are alone but not lonely. *Samadhi* is *vairagya.* In this state we come to know who we are. As soon as we get the answer, we get the solution. *Samadhi* means solution and liberation is attained.

When our nights become dreamless, we enter into '*sushupti'* state. *Samadhi* is when all dreams have disappeared at *wakefulness.* We are in the world, surrounded, but in *vairagya* mode, that is, *samadhi.* When we wake up dreamless, that is *sushupti* and to be dreamless in the day is *samadhi.* When all dreams disappear, that is *samadhi. Samadhi* is when everything disappears and a pleasant emptiness is there. We are alone but very happy. We clearly see the divine in our heart everywhere. We don't have to go anywhere in search of it. We just have to return within our inner self.

*Samadhi* is the state above the mind where thinking disappears. When thinking disappears, all wavering of consciousness disappears also. *Samadhi* means the ultimate state of pure silence, calmness, quietness.

Krishna says:

*'As a lamp in a windless place does not waver, so is the disciplined mind, the transcendentalist, whose mind is controlled, remains always steady.'*

This perfect stage is called *samadhi*. Once established in this state, one never departs from the truth and is never shaken from it. Truth is no theory, no speculative system of philosophy, no intellectual insight. Truth is exact correspondence with reality. Truth is unshakable knowledge of his real nature, his 'self' as soul.

## *Moksha*

It is not possible to describe *moksha*. Generally, people are not inspired by *moksha* because for them heaven is what they want to achieve. People are aware only about *swarga* and *naraka*. They hardly talk about *moksha. Moksha* is when we no longer need to incarnate, or the desire of liberation, the desire to be free from misery and happiness. When we have learnt all our lessons, when we have cleared all our debts, then we attain *moksha*. *Moksha* is the release from *karmic* influences. When we are rid of sin and virtue, when we don't choose right or wrong, that is *moksha*. If we are full of the thought of sin and virtue, then we are full of duality. Happiness and misery, sin and virtue, all will remain when there is duality. When we go beyond this, that is *moksha*. If there is no duality in us, that means we are a *yogi*. *Yogi* means non-duality. We are united.

After creating this mortal world and beings, God remains concealed in them as *jeevatma*, so that they remain bound to the world and carry on their duties and obligations to ensure order and regularity. When human beings are ready for liberation, God uses the power of revelation to rescue them from bondage. This world is called the *chakra*, the wheel. There is the same *chakra*; nothing new; same birth and death, same greed, anger, attachment, same miseries, sufferings. Life is just a repetition. Why go on repeating the same things again and again? *Moksha* means the desire to be free from this cycle, which means we have to get out of this vicious cycle of birth and death.

To attain *moksha*, there should be a perfect combination of *nishkam karma, bhakti and gyana* to achieve completeness. This combination is the ultimate happening. With *bhakti* alone, or *karma* alone, *samadhi* is difficult to attain. With *gyana* we can attain self-realisation and here duality disappears and only *advaita* (non-duality) remains. If we could reach the climax which is the culmination of *gyana* and *bhakti*, then that is the *mandir* of God. *Moksha* is when we want to attain 'God-realisation'. When we search for happiness, it means we want freedom from our misery and that is actually the search for *moksha.*

Knowing 'self' is *moksha*. Knowledge does not mean knowledge of scriptures. When we become what is said in scriptures, then we don't need any rituals, or to read scriptures any longer. That becomes knowing 'self', that is *moksha*. Self-knowledge is *moksha.*

There is no need to run away from the world; only the expectation of the result should end. The expectation for the result is the 'world' and the giving up of the desire for the result is *moksha*. When attachments become meaningless, that is *moksha*. When our inner mind is free and there are no limitations and when we live in *vairagya*, aloneness, this aloneness is *moksha.*

## Sannyas

One who is lost in life and thinks dreams to be true, is a

*worldly person.* He always thinks that he is going to live forever, only others will die and he will never die.

When we understand that death may not be from outside but from within, this understanding means *sannyas.* While living, if we are aware of death, then it is *sannyas. Sannyas* means that this life, between birth and death, is meaningless.

Generally, people take *sannyas* as freedom from family, from society. *Sannyas* does not mean abandoning the house and society and going to the forest. We cannot attain *sannyas*, we cannot reach God by going to the Himalayas, or living in the forest. A *sannyasi* lives in the Himalayas, but is unable to control his desires is fooling himself by hoping to achieve God-perception. Mountains cannot help us in making us a saint, if we do not make effort to find God within. If we are unable to control our *indriyas* (senses), God realisation is impossible.

Nobody can force us to give up the world. Give it up, when you are ready for it. Our outside is not important. Wearing saffron clothes is not important. It is very easy to wear saintly robes. There is no need to cheat and pollute the purity of saffron robes. Don't cheat the world with your fake appearance.

There is no need to leave the world to become a *sannyasi*. By giving up the world, one does not attain God. If we do our *karma* without attachments, if we are self-less *karmayogis*, there is no meaning of the world for us, even if we are in *grihastha jeevan*. We are very happy and peaceful while living in this world. But if a *sannyasi*, living in the forest, seems unhappy, then it means that his *sannyas* is fake. A true *sannyasi* means detachment, whether in the world or outside the world.

*Tyaga*, renunciation, can make us blissful. Without *tyaaga* there is no *sannyasa*, whether we are in the Himalayas or in the *world.*

Control of *indriyas* and mind plays a very essential part in *tyaaga*, in renunciation. If we have no control, we can never transcend from materialism to wisdom. We must detach ourselves from *mohamaya, kama, vasna*, ego, anger, then only we can be *sannyasi.*

*'Detachment is the proof of our* sannyas *in* grihastha jeevan. *For a* karmayogi *renouncing* mohamaya *is the measuring rod for his* sannyas.'

A true sage will not be an escapist because for him there can be no 'this world and the other world'. He will be in the world and not of the world. He will be a lotus flower in muddy water and yet remain untouched by it. *Sannyas* simply means a committed effort to live consciously.

Possession of miraculous powers is not the proof of attaining God. We might gain the power to control the whole universe, yet we find God far away from us. Spiritual advancement is not to be measured by one's possession of magical powers, but only measured by the depth of one's blissfulness.

A real *sannyasi* , whether in Himalayas or a householder *(grihastha)*, will never show us our darkness. We may be a great sinner, but he will never give us a hint of our sins, because that is not worth talking about. A real *sannyasi* understands that we do sinful deeds as we are not aware of our inner potential, our inner self. Rather, he will make us aware about the wisdom , about the light within us, about the Godliness within us.

*Sannyas* means a life which has desire-free action. Usually a man goes to the Himalayas because he has the *desire* for *enlightenment*; so there is *desire* attached. To attain the inner self, we have to be desire-free. When attachment is finished, we become a *sannyasi.* Then we don't need to go anywhere for *sannyas.*

When we go beyond attachment and non-attachment,

that is *sannyas*. Going to the Himalayas or wearing saffron is not *sannyas.* Stay in this world by being detached. The divine would enter 'in' and the world would disappear.

If the mind is calm and stable and we practice *tyaaga*, then there is a greater chance that we will see the truth of life clearly. *Sannyas* is the search of what will not be destroyed. We give up whatever is transient and look for the eternal. '*Sannyas is the search for the* atma.'

By giving up the world, one does not attain God. If we know the *atma*, we know God. Then there is no meaning of the world for us, even if we are in *grihastha jeevan*. Renunciation of ego and not the world is real *sannyas.* No need to leave the world or become a *sannyasi*.

Self- ignorance is world and self-knowing is *sannyas. Sannyas* comes through understanding and this understanding transforms us and without effort our thinking is changed. The world remains the same but inside us, there will be absence of attachment to the world. We cannot receive *sannyas* as a gift from any master. It has to be received directly from God.

Live life in its totality but with total awareness. Then we don't need any outside help. Aloneness is the only thing required and for aloneness, we don't need to go to the mountains. We can be alone even in a crowd. For that we just have to be awakened, be meditative, be conscious, be alone.

Try to find your innermost centre and you can find it by moving inwards.

*And you are a* sannyasi*!!*

## Meditation

*'Meditating on 'Om' can unlock all the secrets.'* When we forget our purpose in life and fall into life's rut, we feel unfulfilled and unhappy. We get depressed and anxious for having forgotten our perspective and losing the way. The

solution is simple. Take the time to remember that we are not here to waste our precious life. Life is so precious that there is no reason to waste it.

India has given the worthiest answer in the form of yoga. India possesses a civilisation more ancient than that of another country. It was Lord Krishna, in a former incarnation, who communicated the indestructible science of yoga to the Sun-god, Vivasvan and Vivasvan instructed Manu (the father of mankind) and Manu in turn, instructed it to Iksavaku (founder of India's Suryavansha), thus passing it from one to another. The royal yoga was guarded by the *rishis* until the coming of *kaliyuga* (materialistic age). Then slowly and gradually the sacred yoga became inaccessible.

Patanjali's yoga is the same science that Lord Krishna gave ages ago to Arjuna and which was later known to Patanjali and other disciples. Yoga is an ancient Indian science.

Meditation is derived from the Sanskrit word *dhyana*. The word *dhyana* means careful concentration, implying an effort on the part of the one attempting to meditate.

The ancient *rishi*, Patanjali defined yoga as '*neutralisation*' of the alternating waves of consciousness. His masterly work, *Yoga Sutras*, forms one of the six systems of Hindu philosophy. When we say 'yoga', it means the system expounded in *Yoga Sutra*, also known as *Patanjali's Rajayoga*.

*'The Yoga system of Patanjali is known as the Eightfold Path.'*

1. *Yama*, moral conduct—non-injury to others.
2. *Niyama*, religious observations—purity of body and mind.
3. *Asana*, right posture—spine must be straight.
4. *Pranayama*, control of *prana* (breath)—subtle life force.

5. *Pratyahara*—withdrawal of senses from external objects.
6. *Dharana*—concentration, holding the mind on one thought.
7. *Dhyana*—meditation.
8. *Samadhi*—superconscious experience.

The inner science of self-control is as important as the outer conquest of nature. Patanjali's *Yoga Sutras* considers the magic of moral purity to be an indispensable preliminary for a sound philosophical investigation. He, who is not willing to observe Patanjali's *Yoga Sutra*, is not seriously looking for inner peace. Its depth, its methods, which include every phase of life, promises possibilities beyond our dream and imagination.

The human can and must liberate himself through inner technique with the help of yoga and meditation. Man can rise even to greater heights, if he is taught the definite science of yoga and meditation. Yoga has a natural universal appeal because yoga science satisfies universal need; thus it does not require formal allegiance. What was once a tool for spiritual exploration, has been turned into a solution for all difficulties or diseases; a cure for all common human problems, ranging from stress to anxiety, to depression. By taking this natural pill every day, we can open ourselves to the potential for countless benefits and there are no ill effects unlike the synthetic pills.

When we stop focusing on external life, close our eyes and are in a relaxed mode, brain activity changes automatically. We are in a state of rest. The brain does not think about external problems; instead there is a new kind of alertness and we don't want to think anything. So, meditation is not to calm the mind; it is to be done after the mind is calm. To achieve this calmness, one first needs to fulfil his *karmic* responsibilities, i.e. perform detached *karma*. In attached *karma*, the flow of life energy is towards the outer world. This way, life energy is wasted. It is necessary first to become a *karmayogi* by performing actions without attachment to their fruit.

A yoga practitioner reserves the flow of life force and is mentally guided to the inner world. By regular practice of meditation, the *yogi* attains calmness, becomes undemanding, prefers silence and wants to stay alone. He discovers that peace lies within. The mind turns inward to experience the 'self'. If we focus our mind while meditating, we notice that the inner world is not a mystery. It may be complex in the beginning but we must stay focused and not go out of balance. Even if the mind is chaotic, we must remain centred. Yoga enables the doer to switch off or on at his or her will. He or she attains the power of sense disconnection. With the advance practice of yoga and meditation, a yoga practitioner can influence not only the effects of past actions (*karma*) but also receive directions from the soul which helps to break the past *karmic* chain. By practicing yoga-meditation, a *yogi* stops decaying of the body by securing an additional supply of oxygen or *prana* (life force).

Krishna says:

*'The* yogi *becomes eternally free, who, seeking the supreme goal, is able to withdraw from external phenomena by fixing his gaze on the mid-spot of the eyebrows and by neutralising the even currents of* prana *and* apana, *within the nostrils and lungs, and control his sensory mind and intellect, and banish desire, fear and anger.'*

In *Yoga Sutra*, Patanjali wrote that yoga consists of body discipline, mental control and meditation on 'Om'. 'Om' is a creative word, the witness of divine presence.

The technique that is especially effective when practicing meditation is to become an 'observer of the mind'.

Meditation starts by being separate from the mind; by

being a witness. This is the only way of separating ourselves from anything. The key to meditate is to learn how to remain unoccupied, which takes a lot of courage. Repeating a *mantra*, or focusing on one's breath is a common practice while doing meditation. But if we remain unoccupied, meditation happens spontaneously. This is the whole crux of meditation —how to remain unoccupied. Then there is no need to do anything.

Within we have created a chaos and our inside is fully cluttered. We have to encounter it and go through it. Courage is needed—to be oneself and move inwards. To be meditative requires great courage. Meditation is when we separate ourselves from the mind and become a witness. Watching is the key to meditation. Watch the mind. When we *watch*, the mind slowly becomes empty of thoughts; but we do not fall asleep, we become more alert, more aware. As the mind becomes completely empty, our whole energy becomes a flame of awakening. This flame is meditation and is experienced by observing, by watching the mind.

Meditation is another name for 'observing' without any judgement or any evaluation. Meditation is a delight in one's own being. It is a totally relaxed state of consciousness, when we are not doing anything. Meditation is not doing anything—no action, no thought, no emotion. When we don't do anything, the energy moves towards the centre and settles down towards the centre; but when we do something, the energy moves out.

Meditation is a simple process of watching our mind and not trying to control our mind. Whatever passes, we simply take note of it without any prejudice. We should not judge our thoughts when we are meditating and think of the ugly thought or the beautiful and virtuous thought because the moment we use our brain to judge our thoughts, we lose meditation. Meditation means remaining unrelated with our thought process and watching whatever passes; only watching and then a miracle happens. We notice that less and less thoughts pass gradually. The more alert we are the more thoughts pass. When we are perfectly calm even for a single moment, all thinking stops immediately and this moment is 'meditation'. Slowly, slowly, these moments come more and more and stay longer. A time comes when we can move into these empty spaces with no effort, whenever we want. They are refreshing and rejuvenating and make us aware of who we are. One cannot be free without being aware and to miss self-awareness is to miss everything. Meditation is only possible through awareness. Unless one transforms one's unconsciousness into consciousness, there can be no meditation.

In the state of meditative silence, *mantra* recitation becomes faint and we reach the stage when we experience complete silence and the *mantras* fade away altogether. Silence helps us to make the inner world completely silent. For the first time, we feel as if the material world has been left behind and now we are in the world where spirituality commands our brain.

Engaged in *dhyana*, the *yogi* sees the self in all and the all in oneself. When the mind has become transparent through the practice of *dhyana*, the true self is revealed and the *yogi* reaches the state of absolute self-contentedness. This is bliss! This bliss transcends the senses. On reaching this state of bliss, the *yogi* realises that there is nothing more superior to be gained now. To reach such a state, even the mightiest sorrow is unable to shake the *yogi*. Indeed, this state means a complete disconnection, a complete end from grief. The *yogi* reaches the final goal of *kaivalya* (absoluteness), in which the *yogi* realises the Truth beyond all intellectual apprehension. If and when oneness with God is achieved, the distinction of various paths disappears, dissolves.

We cannot progress and flourish on the path of *dhyanayoga* if we have not disciplined ourselves. Discipline means, in terms of sleep, eating proper *sattvic* food, *sattvic* thoughts and positive harmonious behaviour.

*'The yogi should constantly practice concentration of the mind, retiring into solitude alone, with the mind and body subdued and free from hope and possession.'*

Krishna says:

*'The mind is restless and difficult to control; but through practice and renunciation, it may be governed.'*

*'Yoga is hard to be attained by one with uncontrolled self; but the self-controlled, striving by right means, can obtain it.'*

## *Vairagya* (Aloneness)

*'When we stay wholly within ourselves, all relationships dissolve.'*

**I am Alone but not Lonely.**

The whole world may be crowded but still every individual is alone. Even when we are surrounded by people in the house, in the society, we feel alone. Loneliness is a lack or a feeling that something is missing; a pain, a depression, a need, an incompleteness, an absence. Loneliness is a negative state. It is possible to be with people and still feel lonely, which is perhaps the most bitter form of loneliness.

This loneliness is unbearable and we want to get rid of it. In such a situation, we can do only two things—either we create relationships so that loneliness can be forgotten or go into solitude, aloneness. As we don't know the art of being 'alone', we tend to go in search of external help. We scour our social circle and the internet for a companion to rid ourselves of our sense of isolation. We go on tolerating this hell or the nonsensical behaviour of others in the name of togetherness. We feel that staying alone is also miserable, then why not tolerate the hell of others rather than suffer the hell of being alone, that is why we go on tolerating the hell of others. We feel it is better to be in the company of enemies than to be left with ourselves.

For the sake of avoiding loneliness, we keep our mind so busy with malicious gossip, meaningless conversation and futile lifestyle that we start feeling being busy. It is not easy to live with another person whose lifestyle is different, whose thoughts or likings are different.

Two different people clinging to each other because they cannot live alone means two miseries making twice as much miseries. We cling to others often out of fear of separation, in other words, we are fearful of being lonely. In that fear we are unable to give to the other the freedom to be whoever they are. We want to control and mould them according to our desire so as not to lose them. When we become attached and afraid, we become stagnant. We are afraid to be on our own. We are terrified of loneliness. We make our own world because loneliness hurts. We try to fill this loneliness with money, with friends, with family.

Fear-oriented life can never lead to peace and happiness. If we cannot live alone, how can we live with others. We are looking for company because we are not happy. When two unhappy persons meet, how can they give happiness to each other.

The real issue is we cannot get even five minutes for ourselves to relax in the true sense. We cannot stay silent, peaceful and absolutely empty for an hour. We have no time for ourselves to think why we are lonely, despite being surrounded by others. We are happy being dependent on others for our loneliness and we don't mind living in hell. We should know that this path would not take us anywhere and should know that false relationships are just an illusion and will not help us to get rid of our problem—loneliness.

If we are absolutely contented on our own, then why should we need any relationship? When we are happy alone, when we can live with ourselves, there is no need to go in for a meaningless relationship. This does not mean that we will not be able to relate; but to relate is one thing and to be in a relationship is quite another.

A relationship is a kind of bondage, while relating is sharing. We will share our joys with many people, but we will not be dependent and will not allow anybody to be dependent on us. Do not surrender to a person because you feel lonely, because that relationship may be just out of fear and may not have anything to do with love.

Ask yourself, What is missing inside me that I need to get from others? Why do I think I cannot be happy unless I receive acceptance from others? Why can I not give myself what I need from others?

We should find time to be alone, look inside, contemplate over our needs and wants and give ourselves what we usually look to receive from others. Instead of searching for someone else to fill our needs and inner loneliness, we should turn our attention inwards and try to understand what is missing inside us that we cannot give to ourselves. Maybe we are trying to possess someone, or we are dominating someone. When possessiveness is there, everything becomes dirty, ugly and inhuman. When possessiveness is not there, the relationship has a beauty of its own.

We should not depend on others for our happiness. We must try to be self-reliant. Self-reliance will make us our own master. We become respectful in society. We live in hell when we are dependent on others because we continue to feel lonely. If we become absolutely empty, absolutely peaceful even if only for an hour, every day, we will experience calmness within. Don't look for happiness outside.

## Heaven is Within Self

*'Difficult situations offer a way to be spiritually strong by practicing solitude.'*

Solitude is the state of being alone without being lonely. Solitude is a desirable state of being alone where we provide ourselves wonderful and sufficient company.

Aloneness is a positive state, a very constructive state to engage with oneself.

Aloneness is presence, fullness, aliveness, joy of being, overflowing love and bliss.

Solitude is something we choose as it restores the body and mind, while loneliness depletes them. Solitude is a time that can be used for inner search and inner growth which lead to self-awareness.

Aloneness helps to create such a relationship with ourselves that there is no need to have a relationship with anyone else. Aloneness makes us fulfil ourselves. There is nothing lacking in us. We are complete. There is no need for us to go anywhere. There is no need to have a relationship with anyone else when the inner world is so complete.

*'When we stay wholly within ourselves, then all relationships dissolve.'* This stable state is a very fortunate state. It's not something to be unhappy about. Now we can live alone and it is called '*real living*'. If we cannot live alone, how can we live with others? The more we accept being with ourselves, the more we will be able to find that loneliness is not loneliness, but aloneness. In loneliness, we miss the presence of others, while to be alone means that being oneself is enough. It means we have fallen in love with ourselves.

## Loneliness is Painful while Aloneness is Bliss

If our inner is full of chaos, we are lonely then we will face only suffering. The moment we become detached and accept solitude within us, we will start seeing the life within. Suffering and joy, both are hidden within us.

Solitude means to be in love with oneself. It creates such a relationship with oneself that no need is felt to have a relationship outside oneself.

Solitude makes one blissful and complete. Consider yourself fortunate that you no longer desire any relationship.

If there is pleasant emptiness within and completeness without, when all our inner paths are lonely, then we must know that the destination is not far away.

When we experience bliss, ecstasy, it means we have entered *vairagya*. *Vairagya* means that we have accepted loneliness.

This is *sannyas* without going to the Himalayas or without leaving this world. We live in this world, but we are a *vairagi*, a *sannyasi*. A *vairagi* is absolutely satisfied because this has become a *vairagi's* nature.

Relationships are just formalities for a *vairagi*. They can be necessary in this world, but not for the inner world. In the inner world, we cannot go with our relations; we can go alone only. When we are alone, there is no attachment; when there is no attachment, the mind is stable.

This stability is the *ultimate experience*. In this state, we come to know who we are. As soon as we know who we are, we find the solution to our miseries.

We need to experience solitude, aloneness to deal with difficult situations in our life. There is no substitute to living in solitude. Emphasis should not be on searching friends to overcome loneliness but to enjoy aloneness.

- *Happiness surrounds our inner sky.'*
- *Search for bliss within than outside.*
- *Loving self is the first step to develop love towards others.*

## Om

'I am in this world yet I'm not there. There was nothing existent before *me* and there is nothing existent after *me*. And at the end of *mahapralya*, I'll be existing and nothing else will. I'm in every creation but none is in me.'

'Whatever is seen as creation is nothing, but an illusion created by my *maya*. It is like the reflection of a moon in a pond, which makes one believe that there are two moons, or like the *graha* Rahu, which even though present among the *grahas*, is not visible as it does not shine like one.'

'The entire *jagat* is *mithya, maya* and only the Brahma is *satya*. It is only truly existing.'

All those who are searching for the Absolute Truth will end their search with the knowledge that the *Paramatma* resides in all living beings in the form of *atma*. The *atma* is the Truth which one is seeking to find.

***OM, TAT, SAT***

□□□